The Great Splonjini

And Other

Short Stories

EDWARD CLUTTEN

ISBN: 9798838438812

Other publications by the same author:

'All For The Greater Good'

ISBN: 9781549947971

A murder mystery involving a newly-discovered Henri Matisse painting and an odd set of Cluedo characters

'Legendary Stuff'

ISBN: 9781973590651

An irreverent take on stories from the Bible, Greek mythology, English legends and the American Wild West

To Ros

This book is a work of fiction. Names of characters, organisations, places and events are either the product of the author's imagination or are used fictitiously. Any resemblance to actual persons, living or dead, events or locales is entirely coincidental. The spelling is British English except where fidelity to the author's rendering of accent or dialect supersedes this. The right of Edward Clutten to be identified as author of this work has been asserted by him in accordance with the Copyright, Designs and Patents Act 1988.

CONTENTS

Marlon has a flair for doing magic tricks. He teams up with a girl at school, and together they perform an illusion for the end-of-year concert. They meet up again years later. Will they now pull off the most audacious of art heists?

Classical music buff Margaret is persuaded to go on a skiing holiday in The Pyrenees. Will she find true 'amor' on the slippery slopes?

An American professor of literature holidays in the UK to research his ancestry, unwittingly stepping into the pages of some classic English novels.

The somewhat overweight Claudette becomes a model. A budding French artist comes of age.

ACKNOWLEDGMENTS

The Courtauld Institute of Art,
Somerset House, Strand, London.

City of Westminster Planning Authority
Westminster City Hall, London.

The National Gallery,
Trafalgar Square, London.

British Library, Euston Road, London.

Dartmoor Prison Museum, Princetown, Devon

Christie's, Rockefeller Center, New York.

The Louvre, Rue de Rivoli, Paris.

"Dr No" (1962) directed by Terence Young

THE GREAT SPLONJINI

Nothing is more sad than the death of an illusion (Arthur Koestler).

Never ignore the bloomin' obvious (The Great Splonjini).

1/14

"It's wrong to split an infinitive."

"Who says?" Marlon counters with sullen defiance typical of a just-turned-teenager.

"Mr. Ballantyne, our English teacher."

"Why?" challenges Marlon, being older and stubbornly provocative.

"Cos," says Alice, being of a more tender age but feisty with it.

"If I want to boldly split my infinitives, I'll do so, ad infinitive infinitum. Bollocks to Mr. Ballantyne," decrees Marlon, inducing a despairing grimace from Alice, who disapproves of her big brother's grown-up language.

Marlon continues: "Did he tell you *how* thoroughly to obey the rule, or how to *thoroughly* obey the rule?"

Alice was way too young to appreciate the nuances of Marlon's hypothetical query, vis-à-vis the ambiguity of meaning it exploited. And Marlon well knew she neither understood nor even cared. But he posed the question anyway, as if rehearsing for some future debating scenario where he might be in the company of his peers, rather than that of his cute little sister.

"You're talking poo," Alice retorts. Marlon ruffles her hair. Alice takes a swipe. Marlon holds her at arm's length. Her own arms are not long enough to reach him. Marlon laughs.

Though Alice's brother at times appeared monumentally oik-like depending on the rebelliousness of his mood, he was totally devoid of malice, and more than capable of showing enthusiastic affection. However, the adult jury was out – some would remark that Marlon was 'gifted beyond his years', while others, less generously, would observe he seemed 'too clever by half'. Objectively though, one couldn't help but marvel at his natural creativity and thirst for knowledge.

Standard children's fare had never much appealed. Seldom was he able to appreciate junior entertainment, and he disparaged fantasy stories – the wicked witch would whack her wonky wand on the wallaby's whatsit and turn it into a wildebeest... yeah right, he would say scornfully, happens all the time... imaginative plot line... how does it work then?

He did however adore his young sibling, though at the same time dismissed her as an unfortunate goody-two-shoes taking on board everything her teachers told her, and digesting all the fairy tales fed to her by child-centric TV channels as if they were the essential sugar-of-life, to be consumed without question. Whereas in Marlon's world, all things were questionable. He liked to think 'outside the box' – an expression he had recently picked up and would deploy mercilessly until it became hackneyed enough for him to deride instead.

Thus evolved his life, every success being tucked away as nothing more than a fond memory, yet every failure an experience from which to learn, and put towards new successes. And failures there were, and painful too. Marlon would often recall a series of setbacks he experienced when he himself was Alice's age: His junior class had been confronted by a large water-colour painting of a riviera-like seaside town. Miss Sturgiss had pinned it to the whiteboard. A majestic old steam engine, billowing smoke, was hauling a passenger train along tracks which could hardly be any nearer to the seafront without impinging on the silvery sand of the beach itself. Marlon faintly recognised the general depiction, having holidayed with the family a couple of times at his aunt and uncle's posh house in Devonshire.

A large picture. Plenty of detail for Marlon to get to grips with. But painted freestyle, rather than copied faithfully from a photograph, he decides, because there are no obvious signs of realism – no litter, no high-sided lorries obliterating otherwise impressive facades of buildings, no dogs fouling pavements, etc. And the passenger coaches are being pulled from right to left, as viewed from the sea (not a convenient place to set up a tripod or easel).

Miss Sturgiss is in command. Where is the train going? Hands up those who think they know. And the patronising tone of the young schoolmistress (despite all teachers being regarded by children as obviously very old) sings encouragement to all the little darlings as they strive to puzzle it out.

Marlon racks his brains. If he remembered right, it was a King or Castle class locomotive, as used on the famous old Great Western Railway. There was no seaside on the way to Bristol. Therefore, it could well have been Devon or Cornwall or somewhere, Paignton or Torquay maybe, no wait – didn't the tracks run along the promenade at Dawlish? Marlon examines the shading, trying to work out from the position of the sun which way the engine was travelling.

Maybe it was North Devon, and the train was heading back towards London, for Waterloo, or would it be Paddington? He continues to search for clues, while keeping his arms firmly crossed. Many hands are being raised. What had others seen that he hadn't? Even daft Millie Arbuckle is excitedly fidgeting, with her hand in the air.

"Marlon?" Miss Sturgiss teases, delighted to find Marlon the only child with hand still down. But Marlon didn't do panic. Panic was for people who couldn't figure things out in a rational way. He merely shakes his head.

"I'm really disappointed in you Marlon."

"Sorry Miss, I don't know."

"Well, *really* Marlon. All together children... What do we think?... We think... It's going... to the... STATION!"

Anyone who was too clever by half might have blown their top at that point. Of course it was going to a wretched station somewhere – any silly idiot knew that. But blowing tops or even using impolite adjectives is not Marlon's public style. He is too clever by a lot more than half. He lets it ride, sits pretending to be embarrassed, and registers the lesson learnt: never ignore the bloomin' obvious, no matter how blindingly banal it may be.

"True but useless," decides Marlon. It was like

asking your doctor why your knee hurt. 'It's because there's something wrong with it,' the learned man of medicine might reply. True but useless. That was to be Marlon's catch phrase from then on. Until he got tired of it, of course. The little Jewish boy in the class puts his arm round Marlon's shoulder at play-time.

"You OK, matey?" Leslie enquires with genuine concern. "Not like you to let Miss Stodgy get the better of you."

Les was nice, cheerful, and thoughtful. Les was going to be Marlon's best friend from then on. Les qualified to be shown one of Marlon's magic tricks. Les was honoured – though he didn't realise it at the time.

And after lunch the very next day, Marlon raises the end of a refectory trestle-table using the empty shoebox in which he had brought to school two coffee tins.

Marlon places one tin on its side, then releases it so it rolls down the inclined table-top. Marlon then offers Leslie the other tin: "Bet yours can't do that," he challenges his latest soul-mate.

"Do what?" says Les.

"Roll down the table," says Marlon.

"Well, blimey, matey," protests Les, "Cos it will."

"Go on, then," says our junior sorcerer.

Les sighs, bemused. Les decides to humour his school chum, Les being nice like that. So he takes the second tin, places it on its side and lets go. The tin rolls down the slope.

The tin then rolls back up the slope.

"Whaaah!..." cries Les, who bursts into hysterical laughter.

"Try it again," says Marlon, "perhaps you didn't do it quite right."

And Les does it again, and it rolls down again, and it then rolls back up again. It was almost too much for the little lad to handle. "You've got a jumping frog in there, matey," he exclaims with glee.

"No frog," says Marlon. "Just magic." Les wants everyone to see it, but Marlon is not so keen, adding, "It's secret magic – just between the two of us."

"Whaaah... no matey... how???..." Les is desperate for an explanation, like people always are when they witness magic. "It must have a motor in it, for sure. Is it electric?"

Marlon had manufactured the trick over the previous weekend, deploying a sturdy rubber band stretched between hooks glued to the inner centres of the lid and bottom of the tin, and a spent six-volt square battery, as a suitably heavy weight, taped to the middle section of the elastic. Marlon was pleased that he could innocently declare it had a battery in it. (True but useless.)

The simplicity was sublime. When the tin rolled down the slope, the elastic, constrained by having to support the weight of the battery, twisted, slowing the tin to an eventual stop, whereupon the elastic would unwind, rolling the tin back up the incline, as if bouncing. Marlon was pleased with Leslie's enthusiastic disbelief, especially after having tried out the trick at home on a much younger Alice, whose disappointing but predictable response was, "So what?"

"What say we go find some real frogs at the weekend?" Marlon suggests to his bosom buddy and willing captive audience. "I know a fab spot down by the river."

And on the following fine Saturday morning, Marlon duly calls at the home of his friend, where Mrs Goldstein opens the door and is puzzled to find adorning her front step a confident bright-eyed boy with empty jamjars. Can Leslie come out? Oh no, I don't think so. An admonishing shake of the head. Not at all, I'm afraid not. Bye bye.

Marlon is perplexed. He hadn't been rude. Admittedly, he wasn't dressed in his Sunday best togs, but who would be if they were intending to go larking about in the river mud? Not any explanation. Maybe Leslie had something more pressing to attend to? But what could possibly be more important than catching frogs by the river on a passably bright Saturday morning in late springtime England? Conundrums rarely flummoxed Marlon for long, but the explanation of this one not only took an age to understand, it took a deal longer ever to accept.

2/14

But all that was then. This was now. And Marlon was in the final throes of secondary education at the comprehensive school, where neither a stultifyingly bland syllabus nor school administrators' rejections of streaming and specialisation had succeeded in moulding him into the amorphous model of employable young adult required, supposedly, by the modern world of commerce.

Despite all this, he was happy, confident, ambitious, and popular. And, not least of all, temporarily he was The Great Splonjini.

He, ably abetted by the beguilingly beautiful and lusciously lovely (according to the programme) Mandy with the wild flowing red hair and amateurishly-sequined ill-fitting leotard (not mentioned in the programme), would be headlining the sixth-form review, a regular end-of-year concert in the school hall, eagerly anticipated by pupils of all ages, teachers, and parents.

Mandy, a live wire, was the nearest thing to a girlfriend Marlon had yet experienced, and together they had devised and practised some routines to perform for an audience who, frankly, would not be expecting too much, corny jokes and risqué innuendo being the staple of this particular annual event. And if their double act fell flat, no one would shed any tears. But it wasn't going to – Marlon was determined to go out with a bang, and he had already prepared a black balloon with "BOMB" written on it in large white letters, filled with confetti and with a sparkler carefully loaded through the knot of the neck, ready for ignition.

Marlon, The Great Splonjini, would entertain them, amaze and perplex them, make them laugh, make them wonder, and enthral schoolchildren of all ages. And, he hoped, many of the grown-ups too, who having politely and appreciatively endured the school orchestra's dodgy rendition of Vaughan Williams sea shanties, a badly-timed yet hilariously messy custard-pie-throwing sketch and a rather embarrassing performance of Monty Python's Lumberjack song, would by now be showing signs of restlessness in the assembly-hall's less than comfortable seating.

"Laydeeez and gentlemen, boyzz and girls..." he begins, then adding some junior humour: "And anyone else not covered by those descriptions..." (Titters from the assembled throng). "I give you my attractive and talented assistant Amanda..." (Mandy twirls, audience claps). "Well, I don't want her any more..." (Titters, again).

Truth was, Marlon did want her very much, but at the time was afraid to admit it. He held in high regard such occasions whereby boys and girls got together for the purpose of being creative. Relationships were surely better forged by intellects combining for a common goal rather than people being awkwardly thrown together in artificial environments like parties or dances. Unless, of course, dancing was your thing. Despite being pleased with this theory, he hadn't quite worked out how a quick snog was ever justifiable when you were co-scripting clever dialogue, yet was practically inevitable and perfectly excusable when you were slow-smooching to Dr. Hook with the lights turned dim.

But right now, humour was key. It seemed to Marlon to be an essential weapon in the illusionist's armoury. Not only did it get the audience a little off-guard, it heightened the effect of the trick, by creating a wider chasm between the comfortable acceptance of the laws of nature, and the sudden alarm that somehow the dark arts may have sullied those sacred rules. Like a round tin rolling uphill.

"A pure white dove, you say?" asks Splonjini.

"Yes please," Mandy confirms.

"But, how romantic," says Splonjini, producing a bundle of patchwork rags uncannily resembling a dead pigeon from the voluminous sleeve of his flowing robe. The fake bird is tossed into the front row. (Gasps, screams, laughs.)

"And now my alluring assistant will blindfold me, then move amongst you and get you all to select a playing-card from her pack, whereupon I shall by the miracle of thought transference announce the value of the said card which you each have picked. Amanda, if you please."

Mandy ties the blindfold on Marlon. Marlon acts suitably blind. Mandy tosses an expensive-looking vase into the air. (Gasps.) Marlon stretches arms out and catches it. (Relieved laughter.) Mandy ties on him a blacker-looking scarf and sets off into the audience, walking like a very grown-up girl indeed, Marlon observes through his new but equally-ineffective blindfold. Mandy shuffles the pack, competently and ostentatiously. It doesn't make any difference to the trick of course. Brown, a third-year boy is the first to pick a card, any card.

Mandy shows the card around to those close enough to be able to eyeball it, and shields it from the stage.

"Oh, tremendous Splonjini! Use your great powers to tell us the card J M Brown has randomly chosen," calls Mandy.

"I can't see..." Splonjini despairs, though it doesn't matter if he can see or not. "No wait... It's coming clearer... The Three of Spades," the great (blindfolded) mindreader replies. Youngsters in the audience fall silent in genuine awe, older ones silent with suspicious awe. It's a put-up job, some concur knowingly, though all magic, of course, is a put-up job.

"Now, greatest conjuror! A new card for you to identify!" Splonjini's delectable assistant calls out, having invited another audience member to participate.

Splonjini appears to hesitate, is he unsure? No, he's certain. "It's the Eight of Clubs!" Splonjini does it again! How does he do it? Even some of the teachers are raising their eyebrows.

"Oh miraculous magician, another baffling playing card for you to ponder and identify, if you would be so kind," requests Mandy, improvising old-fashioned music-hall expressions evermore adventurously as she goes along.

"Don't over-do it, doll," Marlon is thinking. "Just keep your mind on what you're doing." Splonjini comes up trumps again: "I think it could be... yes... the Jack of Diamonds." (More gasps, whispers and claps.)

Mandy reshuffles and invites stiff-collared Mr Ward to join the fun. Splonjini wonders if Mr Ward, the history master, full of facts, dates, wars and peaces, but devoid of common sense or logic, would twig it. No chance. You were more likely to be undone by young children, Marlon reckoned. Somehow their sense of reasoning was potentially clearer cut than a grown-up's, which would be muddied by years of different experiences and their explanations. "Oh magnificent wizard," Mandy calls, following it up with the customary rhetoric, blah, blah, blah...

"Could it be... yes, I think it is... the Seven of Hearts." (Enthusiastic applause.) They perform just a few more – no need to milk it, Marlon had advised his co-performer. It was like shelling peas. Taking candy from a baby. Give Mandy her due, she had learnt the conventions well. And that sparkly leotard she'd (almost) squeezed into was efficiently sapping the concentration of several among the older boys, not to mention the male teachers, Marlon suspected, reminding him of the pickpockets' time-honoured dictum: 'When the fluff saps the mark, the dip rips the wad.' And Mandy was as fluffy as they came.

At which point, Marlon, the (three)mendous (S)plonjini, the gr(eight)est of (C)onjurors, the mir(Jack)ulous (DiaM)agician, the magnificent(seven) of wiz(Hearts), and so on, and so on, begins the build up to his grand finale: "You are witnessing the Great Splonjini, master of the art of delusion and messing about in art class."

Oh how they now tittered and giggled, especially the younger ones, on whom the delusion malapropism was almost certainly wasted. Several older ones snigger, heckle or contribute reasonably good-hearted jeering. Grown-ups, who normally would be sitting ready to stifle a wince as their charges or offspring would inevitably do something crass, are watching now with genuine fascination. Splonjini wheels onto the stage his 'magic disintegrator' – a flimsy construction the size of a telephone box, a frame of balsa wood with cardboard panels, and with a bed-sheet for a door flap. It is laughably Heath-Robinson, capable of accommodating no more than one person and with no possibility of a secret compartment or a secret anything. And the stage itself has no trap doors.

Then he makes the headmistress disappear.

3/14

But that was then. Now was a quiet, neat, flower-decked but soulless cubicle in a Hastings hospice. Marlon's father lay terminally ill. Marlon, now well into his twenties, knows this is the last time he will see his dad. They were of course, father and son, but somehow they had never seen completely eye to eye, making what were trying times for anyone, more difficult still.

When much younger, his father, an automotive engineer by trade, had taught his son how to use tools properly, to be neat, tidy and economical, and to make and repair things. Marlon would quickly pick up the basics, but would always be suggesting other ways of doing it or taking short-cuts. Marlon was always excited about the future, whereas his father never seemed excited about anything, other than grinding out an existence based on the working-class conventionality which he claimed had always done the family proud.

They had recently fallen out over some money Marlon had inherited from his uncle in Devon, who had died a widower and bequeathed his substantial estate to the various young relations, including Alice. Marlon ignored advice to put the cash, a tidy sum, into a building society as a nest egg for a rainy day. His father castigated him for squandering it in a foolhardy business venture and gambling recklessly on stocks and shares.

However, they each tried to put aside their differences, and talked about things that had occurred in their respective lifetimes. Marlon described some of the occasions where he had performed tricks using props his dad had helped him design and build, adding that opportunities for doing magic these days were becoming few and far between. Conjurors were not even being hired for childrens parties any more. Why would you, when you can simply inflate a bouncy castle and lay on some burgers and a bucketful of popcorn?

Then, something his dad said, struggling to get the words out, shook Marlon cold: "So... how did you make... that teacher woman disappear, son?"

It seemed an age since that episode. It had never been discussed at home – both Marlon's parents worked full-time, never attending school functions. The preparation of the props, including his 'disintegration chamber', had been done hurriedly in the school's workshop. Alice had attended the show, somewhat under duress, but as far as Marlon was aware, the event completely passed his mum and dad by.

"At the school concert? Dad, that was years ago – you weren't there. I didn't think you even knew anything about it."

"Shop stewards... called us all out that day..." his father recalls, his voice deteriorating.

"Couldn't face... going home telling your mum... the paypacket was going to be light... went to see your last school day instead... sorry, never got there very often, did I?..."

"Dad, I never knew. You've had all this time and you never mentioned it before. That trick? It was a simple switch. Thought someone like yourself, an engineer and everything, would have sussed that out in no time."

"Why I never... asked you before, son," his father tries to explain, hardly able to find breath to speak. "Didn't want you thinking... I was dim..." Marlon was horrified by the realisation that his own father revered him to the extent of feeling shame or intimidation in his presence. His own father. What sort of monster was that father's son?

Marlon's sad, clouded thoughts travelled back to that day in the school hall. He tried to picture his father, sitting unobtrusively somewhere at the back, uncomfortably watching his son make a spectacle of himself. The austere Mrs Bullock, the girls' headmistress – Mrs Tweedy as Marlon and Mandy had dubbed her on account of the dowdy two-piece outfits she wore. She of the mud-coloured tights and ever-sensible shoes. And the slim attaché case clutched closely to her bosom at all times. The illusionist's 'Pledge' – the normal everyday object. Who'd have thought it? Who'd have given it a chance that someone of her standing would allow herself to be associated with such a naff stunt, the brainchild of a rough diamond from the boys' sixth form. Recipe for disaster, surely?

Even Marlon had been surprised, although he had optimistically written to her beforehand, using the most respectful prose he could muster, explaining in detail how the illusion would act out, and how the strength of character shown by her participation would be an inspiration to all the developing girls in her charge. He had added the polite request that should she decline his proposition in deference to her own authoritative maturity (the vanity card that came up trumps, Mandy suggested), then please would she kindly keep the details under wraps.

But Marlon never had cause for concern. Mrs Tweedy was not only up for it, she played her part like a seasoned pro. Almost too well, in fact, remaining doggedly in her seat for a worrying amount of time after flatly refusing the Great Splonjini's call for a suitable disintegration chamber subject. Splonjini, as arranged, tries one more rallying call to the youngsters in the forward seats who chant Mrs Bullock's name even louder, gleeful at the prospect of the disintegrator ridding them of their fearsome nemesis, while, of course never seriously believing Splonjini's cardboard machine would actually do the business.

His dad, along with hundreds of other pairs of

eyes would have watched intently as a reluctant, nay miffed-looking Mrs Bullock rose from her side-aisle seat, walked down to the side of the stage, up three or four steps, across the back of the gathered stage curtain, then two or three paces and into the box where Splonjini, like a chivalrous gentleman, holds open the flap. The ill-fitting bedsheet serving as the door seems amateurishly positioned, such that it awkwardly casts a shadow over the lady, but there is no mistaking the tweedy skirt, the thick tights and those sensible shoes as they step inside the ridiculous enclosure. And, of course, that trademark briefcase! And neither is there any mistaking that stern, politely impatient voice enquiring, "This won't take up too much time, I hope, Mr Splonjini?"

Splonjini enacts a few passes, drumming up audience participation reciting spells and doing countdowns, each time opening the flap an inch, observing a non-empty box and quickly re-shutting it and acting worried. He would wait. Draw out the suspense. Get them jeering. Let the suspicion build up that it all was going to be an inevitable anticlimax (but more specifically, to allow his accomplices time to play their respective rôles). Then finally, the last resort – the bomb (marked 'BOMB!'). (Laughter.)

Using a cigarette lighter, he sets going the sparkler. The tension (gasps, breaths held). The 'Turn' – making something normal do something un-normal. Splonjini lobs the balloon over the side panel and into the disintegrator. There is an anxious delay – had Mandy not found the pin? Relief. Bang. Confetti everywhere. Sides of box crash outwards and smack the stage floor. In a more-glittery-than-ever leotard, a beguilingly beautiful and lusciously lovely girl with wild flowing red hair poses triumphally inside the wreckage of the box. (Stunned silence, followed by rapturous applause.)

"And with that, I take my leave," says the Great Splonjini, bowing. "The evil Mrs Bullock is no more. Gone forever. Disintegrated!" (Cheers.)

And after the cheers subside, the 'Prestige' – normally the hard part, getting everything back to normal. And on cue, marching in sensible shoes from the back of the hall, Mrs Tweedy, brief-case in hand, begs to differ: "Oh no! You don't get rid of me that easily." (Amazement. Whistles. Clapping.)

"You see, dad," Marlon says to his father," she was never in the box. Mandy dressed up in a wig and identical clothes and they switched over synchronously in the second it took to cross behind the drawn-back curtain. Then the school woman says something so it sounds to everyone like she's in the box, then nips out by the fire exit and legs it back round to the front entrance. Mandy, inside the box, strips off down to her cozzie again. All an illusion, see dad?... dad??... dad???..."

4/14

But that was then. Now is another decade on, and the end of the world is looming. But Marlon may be able to save the day.

Only he, and his like-minded geeky contemporaries, are capable of averting the impending Armageddon threatened by the most insidiously virulent infection known to man since the bubonic plague, affectionately known to a bemused non-technical public as the 'Millennium Bug'.

Years earlier, Marlon had drifted into electronics, attracted by the opportunities afforded by miniaturisation and advancements in manufacturing techniques. The advent of multi-layered circuit boards and high-yield semiconductor 'chips' – multi-function microscopic devices fashioned from a silicon substrate, was seriously about to transform the way we all lived. Computers and other robotic devices were no longer the sole domain of science fiction writers, and powerful systems no longer needed to be housed in special environmentally-controlled buildings with false floors to conceal the miles of cabling, and air-conditioning to keep cool the army of operators who scheduled job runs, and fed cumbersome exchangeable discs, tapes and punched cards into peripheral enclosures the size of washing machines. 'Workstations' were beginning to appear on desktops, and not only for work at work – at home too, where enthusiastic users were fast getting hooked, in the same way that Marlon's parents had been when television first intruded into their front room.

For Marlon, the nascent technologies offered exciting new ways to perform magic. Not magic as in theatrical performances – he had long since abandoned ambitions in that direction, but the magic of automation, of knowledge gathering and assimilation, of monitoring, of spying, and of monitoring the spying. Information was power, he believed. Especially inside information.

Back before his father died, he had used his uncle's legacy to set himself up as a 'hi-tech' trading company. What was left over, he invested in an American software company which had recently offered its stock for trade on the open market. The giant computer conglomerate IBM (soundbites: "I think, therefore IBM" and "No one got fired for buying IBM") had inexplicably published the full detailed design specification of its personal computer product into the public domain, allowing manufacturers the world over to produce similar, compatible machines that individuals could afford to own, thus generously spreading the economic benefits across the surface of the planet, while IBM themselves, totally out of character, committed commercial suicide. But one vital link in the chain remained subject to private copyright licence – the software layer required to make every machine capable of executing the same application programs.

Marlon struggled to understand why the business that owned that copyright, with such a nailed-on monopoly, had now made its shares available for the man in the street to buy. The rapidly-expanding world-wide captive market had no legal alternative but to buy its product, and buy it time and time again, whenever inevitable advances in hardware performance and capacity necessitated enhancements in the operating system software. On the basis that the only reason for it was the obligation to comply with federal regulations, Marlon decided to wager several thousand on the fledgling Microsoft Corporation. Never ignore the bloomin' obvious, no matter how blindingly banal it may be.

But that was then. This was now, and there was a date-sensitivity issue raised by the problem that a year represented by only two digits would 'increase' from 99 to zero as the new century dawned. Marlon, pedant to the end, referred to it as the Centennium bug.

Elapsed times pertaining to loans, savings, lengths of service, etc. suddenly would evaluate to minus a big number. Happily however, he and his band of digital-age troubleshooters, via a modicum of reverse engineering on older machines where source code was no longer available, plus thorough vetting of date fields within databases and how access software dealt with them, ensured that the bug became but a splat on the wall.

The World was thus saved. Until 2038 anyway, when according to Marlon, another similar catastrophe – the end of something called Unix time, was pencilled in.

Once he'd seen off his current contractual commitments, Marlon would start taking things easy, he resolved. Pursue some other interests – take up golf or something? See Alice more often? Jack must be eleven or twelve now, and with Jack's father off the scene, Alice's son would surely be in need of some male influence to shape his development. Give Alice more help with her shop, perhaps? In truth, what she really needed was more exposure – a picture gallery and art supplies business out in suburbia was never going to attract much passing trade. A London location would have been far more likely to succeed, but then London rates were prohibitive for modest startup enterprises. Or would Marlon get married, perhaps? No, wait, hadn't he been told golf was really good exercise for people in middle age?

The last moves of the twentieth century endgame played out like an unremitting electrical storm as the technological revolution peaked. Marlon had rarely been short of work, his specialist consultancy services being in constant heavy demand. Not that he really needed the money any more – his uncle's investment having appreciated several hundred-fold in value...

5/14

"So how about we go and have a spiffing time in London, you and me, Jack?" Marlon suggests. "We could do the Science Museum, or the Natural History, go up on the new big wheel near the Houses of Parliament, binge on junk-food and Coca Cola. What do you say?"

Marlon's sensitive and polite young nephew, not knowing quite how to respond, turns to his mother for support and guidance. Alice shrugs. "If you'd like to," she says encouragingly. "If you think you could put up with your uncle Marlon for a whole day, yes, why not?"

Marlon pulls a face at his beloved sister.

Marlon knew the Capital well, having worked there often. His overly-quiet nephew had yet to experience the great metropolis, something his uncle felt needed urgent redress. Marlon therefore mapped out the day carefully, in order to take in the essential sights, plan places to stop, rest, eat and drink, and generally not get over-tired, which is often the mistake people make visiting large cities.

Designing digital encryption algorithms was childsplay for Marlon, compared to keeping a shy pre-adolescent amused, and the day proved hard work from the outset. On the train journey into town, Jack seemed more interested in peering through the carriage window at successive vistas of open Hertfordshire countryside than taking in significant landmarks like Alexandra Palace or the Arsenal football ground. As the train approached the northern entrance to the Copenhagen tunnel, just before arrival at the London terminus, Marlon pointed up to the parapet from which the bodies of each of the eponymous 'Ladykillers' of the classic Ealing black comedy film had been dumped, dropped ignominiously into empty northbound freight-wagons. Jack smiled appreciatively at the story, but of course, it made little sense to him. Marlon hoped the lad would become more animated on arrival at King's Cross station, when they could stop by the magical Platform 9¾, where the more contemporary Harry Potter and his fellow wizards might be seen departing for Hogwarts.

"It's just a dirty brick wall, Uncle Marlon,"

Jack observes, bewildered.

Marlon explains about the magic of film-making, and how illusions can be created by tricks of the camera. At the back of Marlon's mind was the worryingly disappointing reality that Jack was right.

Jack adds, "Mum said *you* used to do magic, Uncle Marlon."

Marlon smiles, working out the image frame sequencing required to transform a dirty brick wall into a working railway platform. "A long time ago, Jack. A long time ago. Let's go do the Tube."

At last, Marlon managed to elicit a glimmer of wonder from his young companion, pointing out the route they would pursue to Leicester Square via the blue Piccalilli Line (as Marlon delighted in calling it). Detecting a hint of success, he tried to teach Jack how to navigate around the London Underground map, imparting far too much detail for the young chap to take in, of course, but tempering the lesson with interesting titbits like the existence of Aldwych station, not shown on the diagram, which was now used solely as a film set, complete with dummy train.

"Uncle Marlon, why does everything go in straight lines? Even the river? That's wrong, isn't it?"

"It's what they call a schematic layout, Jack. It's done to make all the connections clearer. Quite clever really. A work of art."

After a few moments of deliberation, Jack announces assertively: "Mum says to be true art, it has to be free expression."

Taken aback by such a grown-up postulation, Marlon suddenly realised in whose company he was. Alice. The planned visit to the Science Museum was going to be a waste of time. They resurfaced in the Charing Cross Road.

After taking on sustenance at a lively Italian diner where they enjoyed a jolly exercise in how to eat spaghetti in public, our two intrepid adventurers begin to attack the rest of central London, walking down to Trafalgar Square, with its fountains, Nelson's column and voracious pigeons, planning then to wend their way down Whitehall to ogle at 10 Downing Street and on towards Westminster, Big Ben and the seat of government. Leaving the square, Jack enquires what the big building is on the north side.

"That's the National Gallery," says Marlon, wary of their pre-booked flight-time on the new 'London Eye'.

"What's in there?" asks Jack. Somehow, Marlon knew he would ask.

"Oh, lots and lots of dull old paintings and

what-not," Marlon says dismissively.

The look of disappointment on Jack's face says everything that needed saying. Never was the idiom 'a picture tells a thousand words' more relevant. Recalling never being willing to concede that his own father's opinions were worthwhile, and regretting it only after it was too late, Marlon looks at his watch, works out how long they have before their pre-booked flight on the 'Eye', figures it wouldn't matter if they were a trifle late for it, then turns back to confront Jack's doleful expression. "Come on then, let's go do it."

After Madonna of the Pinks, Madonna of the Veils, and the umpteenth Madonna and Child, Bathers at Asnières, Bathers at La Grenouillère, and Bathers at toutes les routes west of Timbuktu, Marlon's concentration begins to wilt. He does however perk up now and again when more familiar exhibits come into view, such as Turner's Fighting Temeraire, Constable's Hay Wain, and where he and Jack now were paused, at Van Gogh's Sunflowers. What puzzles Marlon is his young nephew's obvious fascination for what seems, on the face of it, a thick-oily daubed representation of wild flowers well past their best, stuck haphazardly in a cheap vase.

Happily, the spin-off was that the problem of what to get Jack for Christmas had been solved. Just inside the entrance to the hall, for show, had been a largish easel, with frame to support a canvas, and a stool for parking the artist's palette, brushes and other paraphernalia. Jack had admired it wistfully. Alice would just love something similar in her comfortably appointed lounge, Marlon decides.

It was time to retrace their steps back to the main entrance. Marlon was beginning to wish he had laid a paper-trail. Then Arthur Wellesley's physog smacks him in the eye.

6/14

It is shortly before Marlon was even born, and James Bond, making his silver screen debut, is in deep trouble. Deep, literally.

Agent 007, licensed to kill, accompanied by (the lusciously lovely) Honeychile Rider, is holed up in the suboceanic lair of the evil megalomaniac Dr Julius No. There on display in the villain's aquarial lounge is Goya's portrait of the famous Field Marshal, 1st Duke of Wellington, KG, GCB, loads more honourable abbreviations, genuine brick and all-round 19th century British super-hero, aka the Iron Duke, aka Arthur Wellesley.

The screenplay implies Dr No, or one of his criminal tong associates, is responsible for the painting's well-publicised recent disappearance

– a nice topical touch added by the film-makers. But a retired Geordie bus driver knows different.

He, or a younger and fitter appointed operative – his son maybe (since the gentleman himself was well into his sixties and weighed 17 stone), at 4.00am on August 21st, 1961, drives to Orange Street, parks his car, then scales the rear outer wall of the National Gallery with the help of a leg up from a convenient parking meter. He requisitions a workman's ladder which happens to be lying about, positions it under a fifteen-foot high window which happens to be left open, and climbs through into a gents toilet. He ambles along to the top of the gallery's main staircase where the newly acquired Goya happens to be displayed, lifts it effortlessly from the easel and carries it back to the loo, back to his car, and back whence he had come, activating none of the building's sophisticated alarm systems, and attracting the attention of none of the security personnel.

Kempton Bunton must have smiled as he sat in the one and nines at the Newcastle Odeon, seeing one of his personal possessions being exploited in a blockbuster movie. It's a wonder he didn't consider suing – the film grossed over $16M, compared with the £8 a week he earned as a bus driver. It was a similarly incongruous comparison that drove Bunton to 'borrowing' the Goya in the first place – the fact that the UK had shelled out a small fortune to ensure the work remained in Britain, whereas Bunton and low-income seniors like him were being extorted a TV licence fee by the BBC, though they watched only programmes transmitted by Tyne-Tees ITV, which was free to view.

Despite years of high-profile campaigns by national newspapers and celebrities to negotiate with the perpetrator of the theft, who regularly sent ransom demands anonymously to the Gallery demanding sums of money to be paid to charitable causes and to needy television-watching pensioners such as himself, Goya's creation remained awol, the artworld remained outraged, and the Met never came close to feeling anyone's collar.

Although Crab Key suffered a catastrophic nuclear meltdown and collapsed into the Caribbean, Dr No with it, the Goya was apparently unscathed, eventually turning up in a left-luggage locker, albeit sans frame, at Birmingham New Street railway station. And Mr Bunton, probably tired of the whole business, gave himself up, claiming he never intended to keep the picture anyway. No one really believed him, everyone expecting the thief to turn out to be a Raffles-like sophisticated master-criminal rather than an overweight bespectacled sexagenarian. He was sentenced to three months for stealing and destroying the frame, mainly because, as the old-school judge sagely remarked, "We cannot have people creeping into art galleries and removing paintings".

And back to the moment, Marlon and Jack make their way to the Gallery exit, both mentally invigorated by their experiences within, but each in extraordinarily different ways.

As a happier, more relaxed Jack gazes in wonderment at the hazy city panoramas afforded by the daytripping couple's glass bubble as it slowly carves its circular orbit through the southbank sky, Marlon's thoughts, triggered by the recollection of the Goya theft story, are of criminal motivation, modus operandi, operational complexity, human factors, security systems, risk and audacity... and art heists in general. But the detailed planning was not his immediate concern. Like a beacon guiding the hesitant traveller along his way, two events were now pointing inexorably to a deadline – Bunton's escapade in 1961 had been preceded by a similarly notorious crime fifty years earlier, to the exact day, back in 1911, when the Mona Lisa was stolen from the Louvre in Paris. Was August 21st 2011 to be a memorable centenary? There was certainly time available to plan it. For someone.

They round off the day by strolling back over Waterloo Bridge, and taking a little look up and down the Strand, where yet another art gallery catches Jack's eye. The day was drawing to a close. "Next time, perhaps," Marlon promises. "Oh look, there's your mum," he says, pointing to the gallery's decal displaying a famous Manet advertising their collection of Impressionists' works.

Jack smiles, noting the resemblance between his mother and the demure young woman in period costume depicted on the poster. The pair then catch a renowned red double-decker London bus which transports them back to their railway station. Thence home.

7/14

The pile of correspondence on his doormat almost constituted a health hazard.

"Dear Householder," the letter began, "This is to inform you that on the above date, our engineers will be testing the quality of tap water samples at residences in your street..." It went on to explain that there was no cause for alarm, and that it was standard precautionary procedure following replacement of aged equipment at the area pumping station. It reassured all customers that any company representative calling upon them on that day would be displaying identification, and customers were at liberty to double-check their validity by telephoning the number on the top of the letter, etc. etc.

Sneak-thief's charter, Marlon thought. Less than one person in a hundred, having received that letter, would not allow access to their home by someone in a dayglo jacket over-slip, carrying a clipboard, metering device, with id card on a chain dangling from their neck, and introducing themselves with, "Hello, I'm from the so-and-so board, you should have got a letter..." Whereas, without the reassurance of the letter, any number of people might be anxious about doing so, and even risk offence by insisting on telephoning for a positive id.

Anyway, the date of the visit had well passed – Marlon had been away for many months, visiting contacts in the far east, shopping, and tying up business affairs. So he binned the letter, whether it was a forgery or not, and probably wasn't, but how do you tell? He did, however, make a mental note of the useful technique for obtaining less-conscientiously scrutinized access to premises he wished to reconnoitre and bug, on the pretext of health and safety issues concerning their electrical systems.

More spam. And yet more spam. Then, a handwritten letter. It was from Deirdre Bullock. Her mother had passed away. There was going to be a memorial service. Marlon was considered a cherished old acquaintance, and therefore was invited... etc, etc. Deirdre must be

Mrs Tweedy's daughter. Marlon had never met her – she was way above his age-group at school, and was not at the house when he and Mandy visited discreetly to rehearse their disappearing act. Poor Mrs Tweedy. She couldn't have been that old. But Marlon suddenly realised with a shudder how old he was himself. A cherished old acquaintance? He was? Really??

But that date was well passed too. He would have been in the mysterious orient buying up oil paintings. He wondered fleetingly if Amanda was also a 'cherished old acquaintance'. They had lost touch with each other after leaving school. Marlon penned a quick reply to Deirdre's expired invitation, apologising for his being out of the country and offering his condolences.

Nothing edible in the kitchen. Marlon freshened up and got back into his car. What were sisters for?

"Ah, the wanderer returns," says Alice, opening her door to welcome in her well-travelled brother. They hug. Marlon is pleased to see his dear sister looking well, although her eyes still exhibit that downward-looking contemplative air, as though her worry-laden thoughts are elsewhere. She still sports a wide fringe and her mop-top of fair hair is tinged with auburn. They go into the lounge where an artist's easel is conspicuous by its absence.

"How's Jack?" Marlon enquires, not surprised that the easel has been demoted to somewhere less obtrusive.

"Oh, he's fine," says Alice. "A bit full of teen angst at the moment."

"Ah... girl trouble?"

"Something like that," Alice replies. Marlon wonders what else could conceivably be something like girl trouble.

"So, what have you been up to?" Marlon asks.

"Oh, you know, same old. Selling crayons, framing, shifting the odd painting now and again. Trying to get more cash in than cash out. Losing battle I think. Bumped into an old girlfriend of yours at my old headmistress's funeral. You got a mention."

"Ah, yes, Mrs Bullock, God rest her soul. I eventually found the invite in the pile waiting for me on the mat. A mention?"

"Her daughter did the eulogy. Apparently the old dear often fondly reminisced about her one-time stage-acting performance with the Great Splondino."

"She could have got my name right, bless her," Marlon says, smiling. "So, which girlfriend was this, then?"

"Oh sorry," says Alice, gratefully grasping the large trowel being offered to lay on some sarcasm. "Forgot there were so *many* of them. Amanda something-or-other, the girl who helped you with your act. She asked after you."

"Really?" says Marlon, trying in vain to disguise interest. "I expect she's married with six kids by now."

"Um, no, not six. Four kids and two husbands. Hang on, or was it two kids and four husbands? Something like that. Nieces came into it somewhere. She seemed reasonably happy, whatever," Alice says matter-of-factly.

Marlon pictured an 18-year-old girl, a freckly red-head with enormous energy and sense of fun, not quite filled out to full womanhood. He wondered briefly what might have been had they stayed in contact. But he was not one for attending reunions, in general believing that people held dear enough at the time would be people you would make an effort to keep in touch with anyway. The idea that the ravages of time somehow would bring together people who never were compatible in the first place was hard to take on board. However...

"Did she leave her number?"

"What am I? A dating agency?" Alice retorts. "I suppose you want feeding. There's a chilli in the oven. We need to wait for Jack to get home though."

"Right. Sounds good. Where is he? Oh, and what happened to the easel?"

"He knocked it over. Fit of pique. Broke the hinge thing. Sorry."

"We talking about Jack? He hasn't got an ounce of pique in him. Anyway, it can be mended. Dad taught me."

"Yes, we are talking about Jack. You've been away a long time." Alice sounds despondent as she describes her son's personality sea-change from being quiet, calm, and happily engrossed in painting to undergoing depressive moods and fits of aggression.

"That's what lads are like at that age, I'm afraid, sis," says Marlon, trying to sound encouraging while he silently cursed Jack's father for abandoning the family, and leaving the boy without a rôle model. "I was probably much like him when I was his age, but look at me now."

"Exactly," says Alice. Marlon had deliberately set himself up, and Alice took the bait. Hopefully it cheered her up. Marlon felt there was something else going on with Jack, but kept his thoughts to himself.

"Anyway, I brought you back a Van Gogh. Thought it would look good on the easel if you parked it in your shop window. All the rage now, you know, people snapping up old masters."

"Oh, what's that, a print I suppose? I've got several already. Yes, thanks, they do sell quite well."

"Nope. An original oil painting. The Chinese are churning them out at a rate of knots, and they're getting better and better at it. You'd be hard pressed to tell this one from the original. Ho Chi Vincent van Ding I think it is."

Alice smiles. "Not sure I'd be allowed to sell something like that, would I? Doesn't it count as forgery?"

"Nope. Only if you try to pass it off as the genuine original," Marlon explains. "As long as you make it clear you're selling a copy, you're home and dry. You just have to make sure the artist has been dead and gone seventy years and there aren't any other copyright issues. You couldn't sell a Salvador Dali or a Picasso, for instance – they're too recent, but Turner, Constable, or the French Impressionists, you're fine. Must be loads of people who'd like Monet's Garden hanging in their conservatory."

"I can't see the profit in it," confesses Alice, who in truth was not born to be a businesswoman. "Surely the artists must charge a huge amount for their work and time. Doing something in oils is painstaking, not like putting a piece of paper through a Xerox machine."

"Ah, that's the thing," enthuses her technically-obsessed brother. "They're developing processes now that spin off from the 3-d printer boom. They've got spectral analysis stuff to get the colours dead right. They even have software that tracks the direction of individual brush strokes.You wouldn't believe what they're doing. It wouldn't surprise me if the whole shooting match was actually automated before very long. And they can produce pictures to any given scale, handy for people with limited wallspace. Fancy the 'Night Watch' hanging in your khazi? They can even simulate the original artist's accidental thumbprints."

"Accidental thumbprints?"

"Yes. Well, no, I made that bit up. But prices always come down when manufacturing processes start getting automated. Just imagine the sales department: "Good morning, sir. Girl with a Pearl Earring, Vermeer? Oil, 40 by 36cm? Of course. Hang on, I'll just enter the details, OK, running the program now, your picture will be complete, dry, cured, and ready to ship in four hours. How would you like to pay? American Express? That will do nicely, thank you. Have a nice day."

The young child version of Alice would have accused her big brother of talking poo. The present-day, world-wearier version simply nodded, not at all convinced she wanted to be part of Marlon's automated artworld. "I don't know what's happened to Jack."

"Want me to go and round him up?" offers Marlon.

"If you would," Alice gratefully accepts. "He'll be at his friend Oscar's house. Probably lost track of time. Here's the address. I'll ring, tell him to expect you."

Two teenage lads are standing close together on a doorstep, anticipating the arrival of Marlon's car. Goodbyes are said. Jack walks away, turns his head momentarily, hesitates, then continues towards where his lift awaits, engine running. Gets in. Greets his long lost uncle.

"You OK?" his uncle enquires.

"Mmm." Jack mumbles.

"We were getting worried. Your mum's got dinner ready for us."

"Not hungry," says Jack. Marlon drives.

"Is Oscar one of your schoolmates, then?"

"Mmm." Jack mumbles.

"Sure you're OK?" his uncle enquires, again.

"Mmm." Jack mumbles, again.

"What's up Jack? Anything I can help with?"

"No."

"Noticed the easel took a dive," Marlon says, trying to break the ice.

"Sorry. It fell over and broke."

"Get much use out of it?"

"One or two paintings. Bit rubbishy." At least responses were now getting polysyllabic. Progress. Marlon detours down a couple of side roads in order to stop briefly by Alice's premises just off the High Street. "Just want to take a quick look at your shop," he says.

"Mum's shop," Jack says.

"In her name, yes," concedes Marlon. "But I think of you and your mum as a team. She needs you, you know that."

"Mmm," Jack says, unconvincingly.

"And I need you too," adds Marlon, rather recklessly as he hadn't yet worked out a good reason to proffer if challenged. "Got a big job coming up."

It wasn't a direct question, so Jack didn't feel any obligation to answer.

"Look, what we all need is that smashing bloke Jack again. With his chat and smiley face. We all go through periods in life when we don't know what's happening to us, when life seems to be one bit of shit after another. Is it to do with Oscar?" Anything other than an immediate response in the negative, Marlon was going to take as a yes.

So yes it was. Marlon was in uncharted territory, and uncharted territory perturbed him – whichever direction you set sail you were equally likely to ground your vessel on a reef. The only thing you could do was set your tiller to an arbitrary course and hope for the best, so he continued: "You know, when you think people are being shitty, or don't have any respect for you, or ignore you, or say things behind your back, it's more likely to be because you're moody and grumpy and not being sociable, rather than the fact you may be gay, which is OK, pretty commonplace and even fashionable these days. I'm looking forward to your mum's chilli. "

A nonplussed boy's face reddens. A car pulls up outside "Arts Delight". A man with big ideas asks his young passenger for an opinion: "I patch up that easel of yours, we stick it just there, pride of place across the front window, put brushes and what-not on the table beside it, then plonk a famous Van Gogh oil painting on the frame. What do you think, partner?"

8/14

Steve could chat for England. Which was just as well – in his line of work, staving off the effects of boredom was a priority. Not that as a security patrol operative you actually want anything to happen – such things were bound to precipitate tedious form-filling, or even herald danger to life and limb in the worst case.

"Speak to you later," he says into his cellphone. "Got a caller at the gate."

Steve's CCTV monitor displays a lone buttonpresser, who he guesses would be the engineer from the electricity supply company, as per the written note on Steve's duty worksheet for the day.

"Mornin' squire, City of London Electricity Supply H&S," says the cheerful man in the hivis tunic, offering his ID badge and handing Steve an official letter of introduction with a fancy QR code in its heading. "Got a scanner?"

"No, it's OK mate, you're expected. Hang on, I'll open up." Steve swipes a card through the gate's locking mechanism. "Gonna take long?"

"No, 'bout fifteen, twenty minutes, maybe. Just need to check out your supply, residual earth-leakage, condition of appliances and other electrical equipment, make sure wiring and connectors all come within EU regs, and your meter's in order. Basically, verify you're not a fire hazard or any other sort of risk to employees or visitors. Usually find it's a tick in the box job. If you'd just point me in the right directions..."

Steve shows the workman around, indicating the security camera locations, how the infra-red sensors on the doors and windows are mounted, the way the telephones, screen monitors and alarm devices are connected, where the environmental temperature and humidity controllers are housed, and where the main fusebox is.

And as they go round, they chat. And it is too hot to be working, they agree. And Steve is keen to point out the disparity between his workload and remuneration. And the electric man suggests the rates are better, surely, if you work night shifts. And Steve is quick to pinpoint his employer's tactic of reducing overheads by scheduling only hourly patrols who move between different locations, there being no one on site full-time out of hours. And as the engineer tidies the tangle of cabling around the uninterruptible power supply, they discuss other burning contemporary issues, arriving at a satisfactory consensus that Spurs will never get anywhere without strengthening their midfield.

"What is this place, bonded warehouse sort of thing?" the engineer asks casually.

"Galleries mainly, museums and what not. Use us for storage when they're refurbishing... or making space for loan items when they're putting on special exhibitions and stuff," Steve explains. "It's all climatic controlled, so stuff doesn't get damaged or anything. Private collectors stash stuff here as well – more secure than leaving it at home when they jet off to the Seychelles for six months every year."

"Ah, alright for some," the engineer complains. "All lost on me, this art stuff, I'm 'fraid, but I s'pose it boosts the economy and everything." He eventually signs off his checksheet and packs away his hand-held meter. "Can you put your initials on the docket, pal, then I can leave you in peace. Everything seems to be fine. Your company will get a confirmation certificate, and whatnot. Thanks, squire."

"Cheers, see ya mate," says Steve, closing up the steel gate and returning to his front office and cellphone.

9/14

"You're crackers," says the attractive red-haired woman putting down her drink. "But then, you always were."

"You know," says Marlon, "I never realised

how much your beautiful green eyes sparkled."

After laughing out loud and a very short deliberation, she comes back at him: "It's probably because of the eye-watering stupidity of what you're thinking of doing."

They both laugh. "And the quick-witted back-chat, it's all still there," says Marlon, transported by the euphoria of reconnection with his old flame. "Alice said you were getting through husbands like most people get through cars."

"Only two," she protests. "First one was a huge mistake. Like a rusty Triumph Herald. Second one was slightly better. More like a boxy Volvo, kind of. Maybe next time I'll get it right. A Ferrari or something."

"Next time? Does that mean number two's days are numbered? A Volvo MOT failure?" Marlon asks.

"No. Don't get any ideas. Number two still has his uses. Besides keeping me in shoes, he keeps me sane. He is Captain Sensible as opposed to your Brigadier Barmy. He doesn't go around stealing things from art galleries."

"I told you, I'm not going to steal anything," Marlon remonstrates. "It's all an illusion."

"Right," says Amanda. "I'll bring you a fruitcake with a file in it when I visit you in jail."

Time flew by like someone had pressed the fast forward on life's playback machine as they sat together in that cosy alcove of a London pub, reminiscing, laughing, and drinking. All three, probably to excess. Period photographs adorned the walls, embellishing the nostalgia as the middle-aged couple recalled their respective histories. Marlon was so glad Mandy had left her business card with Alice. Ostensibly, she was simply stating that she still existed and was contactable. But it seemed to Marlon almost as though she was challenging him to get in touch. A dare. That's what she was like. And he did dare. That's what he was like.

"You're not thinking of whisking me off to some seedy hotel room, are you?" Mandy suggests, slightly slurring her words as the evening's indulgences start to take their toll.

The thought is exciting, compelling. Make up for past opportunities missed. But is it such a good idea? They had first got together in a previous life, one of youthful innocence and fun. The wonderful evening had been a joyous action replay, the two protagonists considerably older, re-creating their relationship half a lifetime on, the repartee flowing freely as a mountain stream, as it did before. They were great friends. It never went any further then, it didn't need to now.

Brigadier Barmy, slightly worse for wear, crashes out back at his London flat. In the morning, still slightly woosie, he phones Alice for a chat – she was bound to ask sooner or later whether he'd got in touch with Mandy. They catch up with each other's news.

"Don't know what you said to Jack," says Alice. "He seems almost back to his old self."

"Search me," says Marlon. "How's the new shop window dressing coming along? Customers flocking in?"

"Can't say that the till has started rattling louder than usual, but there have been several people come in to look more closely at the oil painting. Mostly to ask why he had a bandage round his head, I have to say. D'oh! And Jack's done a London Underground Map in the style of Salvador Dali, would you believe. Don't know where he got that idea from, but it's really quite good, rail lines and rivers mish-mashed up, tied in knots and dangling all over the place. In oils, too. Not going to sell it though, I love it."

"I want it," says Marlon. "I'll arm-wrestle you for it."

"No chance," says Alice. "Get one of your oriental friends to knock you out a copy. I'm sure Hu Flung Dung'd do you one."

"Easy for you to say," says Marlon, his head swimming. It was good to hear Alice in high spirits again.

10/14

No one knew exactly who, but someone had started a rumour going round that a spectacular art robbery was being planned to commemorate simultaneously the centenary of the stealing of Da Vinci's Mona Lisa from The Louvre, and the golden jubilee of Goya's Wellington being ignominiously kidnapped from The National Gallery. 'Social Media', an Internet phenomenon still in its infancy, was rife with gossip about the threatened heist, and commentary was creeping by default into the otherwise unused inches at the feet of national newspaper columns.

Even a gentleman reader of The Times, clearly one of the many not short of time on their hands, was moved to write in to the newspaper, expressing the hope and expectation that the "custodians of our nation's cultural heritage would undertake every necessary extra precaution to avert any such apocalyptic abomination".

The Courtauld's Institute had less cause for concern than most of its fellow curatorships. In only the spring of that year, it had undergone a major refurbishment of its galleries, situated in a corner of the spectacular Somerset House, a neoclassical marvel standing between the Strand and the River Thames near Waterloo

Bridge, and famous in former times for being the repository of myriad birth and death registrations relating to Britain's families through the centuries.

New lighting, decor, information boards and the most up-to-date of security features had been added. The Westminster planning authority had vetted and passed the proposals, in accordance with the stringent guidelines governing applications concerning buildings of Grade 1 Listed status. They had been generously understanding about the need to hide ugly cabling behind Victorian-age oak panelling, or in new ducts, drilled through solid beams possibly set in place by Inigo Jones himself.

And in order to comply with the fashionable modern principle of freedom-of-information for all, the planning department mandarins had helpfully published the entire fully-detailed floor-plans on the world-wide-web, showing the locations of each individual picture and sculpture, whether the exhibit was 'tagged' (T) and where the tag aerial (Ae) was concealed behind the panelling, whether the exhibit had a weight sensor (W), whether it was in view (C) of any of the many ceiling-mounted cameras, the positions of which were indicated (FE for existing cameras, FN for new ones), or, in some cases, marked on the plan simply with an (H) to designate that the item did not require any protection as it was too high to worry about.

The Great Splonjini would have figured it all out anyway, but the drawings saved him a great deal of work and time. His gratitude was no doubt echoed by underworld blaggards everywhere.

As the fateful day approached, opinion that the impending misdemeanour would comprise some violent ram-raid was being discarded in favour of the idea that some little-known exhibit simply would 'go missing'. This would not, therefore, be something the general public would be likely to get too excited about. The upshot was that when August 21st did arrive, it was all pretty much business as usual, albeit a Sunday.

As a muggy afternoon drew towards a cooler and less frenetic conclusion, the Courtauld Gallery, and museums and galleries like it all over the city, were readying themselves to close their doors to the visiting public. Inventories had remained intact. There were no incidents to report. One or two administrators privately breathed sighs of relief. The whole thing had obviously been a hoax, probably the stupid idea of some mischievous prankster, causing anxiety for officialdom, and raising false hopes for many sections of a public hungry for scandalous titillation.

So, while tourists and trippers headed away from the city's daytime attractions, peace again began to prevail. All was quiet. It had been a typically busy, but uneventful summer weekend.

That is, until an attractive middle-aged red-haired lady buys late admission tickets for herself and two young nieces to cross the threshold of an interesting-looking art gallery in the north wing of Somerset House, intent on studying works by famous Impressionists. But she quickly returns from her first port of call, a gallery on the first floor, back to the entrance desk, exuding an indignant air of consternation.

"Is this like a joke?" she complains.

"Madam?" answers the uniformed entrance clerk, politely.

"They're not the proper pictures. I've paid to see originals, not stupid prints, for Heaven's sake!"

"Sorry madam, I assure you all the exhibits here are..."

But the redhead is adamant: "We've been upstairs, the first room we go into, the first picture we look at... it's supposed to be Vincent van Gogh with his ear bandaged, and it's a print, not even from the original, and signed Vincent Van Hire. They're a commercial vehicle rental company in Hertfordshire. It's got to be some big wind-up, surely?"

The uniformed attendant starts to show some concern, and turns towards his female coworker, who calmly replies, "Why don't you pop up and see what the lady is saying. I'll be alright here for a couple of minutes." They weren't supposed to leave a lone official on the entrance desk.

One or two leaving visitors, including the bearded man in a dark hat who had just emerged from the gents, pass through the exit while the sole lady attendant deals with some more late entries. Her uniformed partner is quickly back on the scene.

"Something's happened," he says, with considerable alarm. "Phone upstairs to security. We need to shut the doors."

11/14

But that was then. Now, three years on, Arts Delight was almost national landmark status. People, often on only a whim, would come from far and wide to shop in the town, boosting the local economy, simply to be able to say they'd seen the infamous 'Vincent Self-Portrait with Bandaged Ear' on permanent display in Alice and Jack's shop window. And of course, maybe make a purchase while they were there – the proprietor's son's talents being particularly in demand.

Alice had lost count of the number of

customers who examined the oil painting, wondering and wondering, could it be the real thing? She was careful to point out the accompanying notice that explained that it is purely a copy, and perfectly legal. She had even had to fend off several sorties by an inquisitive local CID, desperately searching for clues to the mystery of the missing art treasure. Alice was always quick to remind people that her painting was on display in her shop way before the real thing disappeared.

On his tediously long journey back from the far east, where he seemed to be spending more and more of his time these days, Marlon kills some of it by reviewing his situation – always a sure-fire sign you are getting past it. The airliner is nowhere near full, and there has been opportunity to chat up the air hostesses, or flight attendants as they were now referred to.

It is a run-of-the-mill trick, using the card deck provided by the airline for the amusement of passengers. One he'd performed countless times over the years. Shuffle. Glance at the open face of the card at the bottom of the pack...

Immaculately uniformed and stylishly coiffured, Natalia picks a random card from the spread pack – admittedly, not without a modicum of difficulty given the length of her decoratively polished fingernails... she replaces her card face down on the top of the pile, and the jovial, entertaining passenger cuts the cards... and invites the stewardess to do the same... and he cuts them again for good measure. Her card is well and truly buried in the pack. Except that Splonjini knows her card resides adjacent to the card he already has made a note of. The impromptu conjuror fans out the deck, spots his known card and cleverly flicks out the card next to it, trying to land it down the girl's cleavage, although her close-cut fitted blouse doesn't leave a lot of room for error.

He misses. How could he miss? Ooops, and they laugh. But it doesn't matter. What matters is that it's the card that the lady picked. However, it is not. He has ejected the wrong card, the one above his noted one, instead of the one below it. Calamity. The Great Splonjini has failed.

The irony, tempering Marlon's bristling embarrassment, is that Natalia bursts out laughing, as though that was the whole point of the act. And her laughter is infectious. The comedy establishes a mutual rapport more solid and genuine than ever a slick bit of magic would have done.

It was a trivial incident. But a reminder of his fallibility, none-the-less.

Marlon was looking forward to touching base with Mandy again – for a good while he had deliberately broken off contact with various key people, to ensure no incriminating associations could be made by investigative journalists or other relevant authorities armed with names and statements of crime-scene witnesses and potential beneficiaries – specifically, Amanda and Alice.

Not that Mandy was a major player in the caper, although she had been more than willing to play some small part. She simply had to be in the right place at the right time, doing something perfectly normal and reasonable. Which, of course, was to play the fluff, and create that diversion – generate a hubbub of excitement, attracting attendants and security people to the gallery room to stare disbelievingly at the space where a priceless painting should have been hanging, rather than doing what they should have been doing, which was searching the toilets, utility rooms and anywhere else the perpetrator of the felony might have been engineering an escape with a large canvas in his possession.

As it turned out, Mandy's cameo acted out perfectly – Splonjini marches unchallenged through the exit door and away from the scene of the crime post haste. Home and dry. It was when he arrived back at his flat and got shot of the wretched beard, that he found the fragment of synthetic canvas in his jacket pocket. Had he been stopped and searched, it would have been a giveaway. The end. Kaput. The difference between entertaining a delicious young airhostess in the comfort of business class, and manicuring his own fingernails with the file out of Mandy's fruitcake. Cold sweat time.

The fragment. The card trick gone wrong. Why was self-doubt creeping in? In years past, Splonjini would have breezed through the routines effortlessly, every eventuality being taken care of, in total control, confident in his own abilities. So, what had changed?... What did the much younger Splonjini used to say? Don't ignore the bloomin' obvious.

12/14

"What on earth were you doing in the loo, anyway?" Mandy asks incredulously. "Not exactly the ideal moment to get caught short, I'd have thought?"

"I had to get rid of the incriminating evidence, didn't I?" Marlon pleads, matter-of-factly, as they each get stuck into another round of drinks in the London pub alcove they have come to call their own. "Pork scratching?"

Mandy laughs. "You know how to spoil a girl. Oh my God," she suddenly realises in horror, "You're not trying to tell me you flushed Vincent van Gogh down the loo?"

Marlon laughs. "Of course not," he says. "What am I? Some sort of demented philistine?"

"Well, er..." Mandy starts to say, her sentence tailing off.

Even though they got together very rarely, and on this occasion not since the day of the 'heist', whenever they did have a meet-up, it always seemed like a seamless continuation of the last one. Marlon had enquired whether the wheels had fallen off the Volvo yet, and Mandy had understood exactly what he was on about. And no, they were still turning, albeit a little slower.

"I told you before, it was all an illusion," Marlon explains. "Like our old dear departed Mrs Tweedy, who was never in our cardboard box to start with, the real Van Gogh was never hanging in the gallery in the first place, at least not since it was taken down and put into storage while they refurbished."

"So... you stole a fake, and replaced it with another fake," Mandy concludes, feeling pleased with herself for beginning to understand what had happened.

"More or less," says Marlon. "But the first fake was realistic enough for people to believe that the genuine article had suddenly been transformed into a poor imitation. Magic, you see."

"Hang on, I'm lost. So, where's the real one?"

"It's in safe keeping," Marlon assures his lusciously lovely assistant. "Another drink? You look more beguilingly beautiful as the evening wears on."

"What *is* that stuff you're drinking?" asks Mandy.

Piece by piece the jigsaw of Splonjini's greatest illusion gets put in place for Mandy's benefit. Marlon relives his night at the warehouse, the 'secure' building he had entered effortlessly, by remotely activating the gadget he clandestinely installed on his previous visit, thus throwing the mains circuit breaker and disabling the intruder alarm system. During that same previous visit, he had rearranged the priority of critical and non-critical devices which utilised the UPS system, thereby knocking out the facility of continued operation by battery should the mains supply fail. And of course, he had surreptitiously cloned Steve's card key using the widget attached to the underside of the clipboard on which the docket was passed over for signing.

He easily locates the area marked out for 'Courtauld Trust', and just as easily identifies the crate where his quarry is to be found, complete with identification label and gallery location for re-hanging. Spookily, it was all as if they knew he was coming, and wanted to be helpful. He carefully removes the original canvas and places it in protective sheeting. He replaces it with a convincing Chinese-made copy, even better than the one he gifted to Alice, and one specially produced on a synthetic canvas mounted on card pre-printed with the obviously faked photographic version. The top canvas can easily be peeled away from its intermediate backing card. The frame and the main backing remains the gallery's original, complete with provenancing detail, dust and moisture seals, and fixing hooks. Only the security tag has to be replaced, with a suitable dummy – Marlon couldn't risk setting off any alarms come the big day.

"Why go to the trouble of making a daft paper copy? Why couldn't you have just left a blank card?" asks Mandy. "Was that so I could sound off about how knowledgeable I was about art?"

"There is a control room upstairs at the gallery, permanently manned by security staff. They have screens showing the camera views inside and outside of all the rooms. The cameras aren't high enough quality to discern the difference between an oil and an imitation print. However, a blank exhibit would be noticed immediately, and wouldn't give me time to get away."

He doesn't bore Mandy with absolutely all the hi-tech detail, but as he sinks another glass of 6X, he briefly recounts how Vincent manages to disappear into thin air from the gallery 'before their very eyes': He waits for a quiet spell of visitor traffic, then enters the gallery room, pausing to study the Van Gogh, then moving close up to the next painting on the adjacent wall, where he is cut off from the single room-camera's arc of vision. Using his own run-of-the-mill-looking pocket camera, specially adapted to act as a Bluetooth spoofer, he connects in to the room's (FE) surveillance camera, one of the older VSC240 types, notorious for its susceptibility to hacking. Setting the camera's operating mode to 'freeze frame', he walks back to the Van Gogh, checking that he doesn't appear on the security camera's image, which he is able to monitor on his own camera's viewfinder. He peels off the canvas, folds it up, places it in his large inside jacket pocket, returns to the security camera's blind spot and restores its mode to normal monitoring. He then walks casually back into security camera view, out of the room and into the corridor, Van Gogh 'intact', security monitor watcher unperturbed, nothing extraordinary to report.

And the inevitable subsequent exhaustive replays in the control room upstairs would fail to show any abnormal activity, like tampering with the painting. Even if anyone reasoned that the last person to view the exhibit without kicking up a fuss had been a bearded man in a dark hat, there was no visual evidence pointing to his culpability. And once the decoy picture had been torn up and washed away to Greater

London's sewage treatment centre, there was no evidence at all.

It could only go down as an inexplicable phenomenon, and one meriting induction into the Hall of Fame of Great Illusions, was there such a thing. Which there wasn't, because having the workings of an illusion explained in mundane detail invariably reduces the illusion to a sordid act of dishonesty, and unworthy of any sort of fame.

"So..." Mandy begins again. "The Pledge – the Van Gogh with his poorly lug-hole. The Turn – instant transmogrification into a dodgy watercolour. Will we ever be getting the... what was it, the 'Prestige' – where everything comes back to normal?"

"See, Amanda," says Marlon. "You've still got it in you. All those things I taught you. We should have stuck together, you and me, Bonnie and Clyding it around the world. Art heists, bank jobs, jewellery snatches... What a team."

"Hmm," says Mandy, unconvinced, "and finish up full of bullet holes in a Ford Fiesta up Tooting High Street."

"Occupational hazard, doll. A chance you have to take," concedes Marlon. "They're opening an ice rink at Somerset House soon, out in the courtyard. The place will be all lit up for Christmas. Probably be really good. You should take your nieces skating."

13/14

A Westminster City Council street refuse and recycling collection operative, as defined by woolly bobble-hat, hi-vis donkey-jacket and wellie boots, wheels his cart around the perimeter of Somerset House's courtyard, the central area of which has been prepared for the grand opening of the ice-skating season. Sweeping up cardboard boxes, plastic bags, sweet wrappers, cigarette ends and the other assorted detritus resulting from a daysworth of usage by the general public, he glances over at the portable rink, fully assembled, with liner, side panels, and equipment purring away in the corner of the yard, pumping a steady flow of refrigerant to the matrix of cooling pipes beneath the few inches of water. Water, he notes, that was beginning to take on that cloudy opacity of white ice. Job done, he departs the square, his cart fuller than when he started, but emptier of one specific item.

No journey back to his homeland would be complete without visiting his sister, of course, and on doing so, Marlon was pleased to learn that everyone was fine and the shop was ticking over. Marlon had already determined that the business probably needed a reboot. "I brought you a few more old masters to bolster your stock a bit," he announces.

"Oh, that's so good of you," Alice says. "You really shouldn't be going to all that expense. Let me..." But Marlon's hand gesture quickly pooh-poohs the idea she should contribute to the cost.

"And Jack? He OK?"

"Yes, he's fine. Out with a friend at the moment," Alice replies.

"Oscar?" Marlon suggests.

"Oscar? No, no. Oscar is yesterday's news. Debbie."

"Debbie? Right," Marlon says, smiling, and accepting the fact that human relationships were things outside his sphere of expertise.

"Oh, and by the way," Alice says. "Talking of old masters, Jack reckons the Vincent in our shop is real, and you stole it somehow from somewhere before the ones in the gallery, whatever they were, got switched over."

Marlon laughs. "Kids and their ideas," he says. "Where did he get that one from?"

"Something you told him, evidently. That you had a big job lined up."

"Well, fear not, sis," he reassures her. "The bogeys won't be coming to break your door down any time soon."

To Jack's credit, that particular scenario had been one that Marlon had considered, and one that would have worked. But it would have been an audacity too far, recklessly risking Alice being implicated in a criminal activity. As it was, her copy was indeed a 'genuine copy'.

Marlon adds: "Like various other craftsmen through the ages, and builders who leave their initials chiseled into bricks, master copyists always leave their signature somewhere on their paintings, just so there's some unique way of identifying them for ever after. Often, their mark takes some finding though."

"Really?" says Alice, relieved that the prospect of sewing mailbags for the rest of her life was now less immediate. "I'll have to look for it."

"It'll take you ages. I'll save you time. You need a magnifying glass, then look into his left eye. The whitish swirls representing the glint of reflected light spell out 'LS' which are the initials of the Chinese lady who painted it. I've got an idea."

"Oh dear," says Alice, ever the pessimistic alarmist. "Am I going to like it?"

The Savoy Hotel lies between The Strand and the River Thames, upriver from Waterloo Bridge. It has a suite named after Claude Monet, the famous French Impressionist who painted several landscapes of the Thames while staying there, and over the years has been patronised by Hollywood movie stars and world political leaders alike. Churchill was known to have smoked cigars and quaffed brandy in the American Bar. Gershwin premiered his Rhapsody in Blue there in the twenties. Built by D'Oyly Carte off the back of profits from his Gilbert and Sullivan popular operettas, the hotel has a long history of involvement in the arts, even supporting an 'Artist in Residence' programme to promote home-grown talent. An appropriate venue, therefore, thought Marlon, for a celebratory get-together. It is also a short walk to Somerset House.

Thus four souls, bedecked in their glad-rags, dine at the Savoy Grill, in spite of Alice's protests about the extravagance. It is Marlon's early Christmas present for his beloved sister, nephew, and the rather shy but nice Debbie. As an after-dinner treat they would stroll along to see the Christmas tree, the lights, and the decorations around the courtyard where ice-skating would be in full flow. During dinner, conversation inevitably gets round to the subject of Van Gogh and his bandaged ear, and whether the true original would ever show up again. "I expect it'll turn up sooner or later," predicts Marlon. "It's probably been put on ice somewhere."

Somerset House's internal facade looks resplendent with its underlit colonnades majestically overlooking the skating area where silvery blue illumination complements the twinkling lights festooning the enormous Christmas tree. A joyous glow emanates from the whole scene. People are having fun. Marlon spots two young girls, clearly skating novices, who are clumsily making progress around the circuit, accompanied by a woman, of whom Marlon has a rear view only. Though filled out somewhat from the derriere that once had set his pulse racing, he nevertheless recognises the person, her flowing red hair and grace of movement confirming his suspicions. Marlon had texted Mandy earlier: "last hurrah.. prestige.. get your skates on.. 9-ish.. 8 of spades xxx".

Marlon can't be sure about the exact timing – the surfactant should by now have eaten through most of the opaque coating on the protective plastic casing, but such things can't be narrowed down to split seconds... though wait, this is the Great Splonjini. He never fails, does he?

Apprehension begins to distract him. Time is worryingly ticking by. Then... Someone has fallen. A child. They are being helped back up onto their bladed feet, dusted down and encouraged to continue. Other skaters arrive, offering help, pausing at the location. Someone is pointing out something odd. There soon is a general commotion, some shouting and a hum of excitement. More people start to congregate at the point of interest. Even non-skaters are hopping onto the ice to go get a better view. Eventually, even Alice, Jack and Debbie succumb to the lure. Marlon, of course, knows what it is already.

Hermetically sealed inside a rigid synthetic container, an aurally-impaired Dutch Post-Impressionist peers helplessly upwards from the frozen depths of his watery grave.

14/14

But all that was then. Now is some years on, and an ageing man again admires the view of the scintillating Hong Kong night lights from his luxury apartment overlooking Kowloon Bay. His chest pains are playing him up again. He cannot ignore the bloomin' obvious – he knows he is living on borrowed time.

He kisses goodnight Lin Su, his long-term partner, and excuses himself – he needs to lie down. He visits, maybe for one last time, his study, where a sad, lost-looking young girl is serving drinks while bawdy merriment prevails in the background.

He had never had any criminal intent himself,

his wealth having been either self-made or down to luck. His one major lapse had been, after organising the return of the Van Gogh, hanging on to the Manet. (Well, he'd done all the hard work breaking into the secure storage depot, why not make the most of it, and exchange a superlative Chinese copy for yet another iconic masterpiece, one for which he had taken more than a particular liking?)

Though he always privately claimed the painting in his study was not stolen, merely borrowed, he nevertheless felt a pang of shame at his self-indulgence. But anyway, he had made provisions in his will that Édouard Manet's beautifully enigmatic portrayal of life in that most famous of Parisian nightspots be returned to its rightful owners after his death. It would be his gift to Britain, the land of his birth, with thanks for letting him be the painting's custodian for so long. And after all, as far as he knew, no one had yet missed it. An ambiguous gesture, maybe, but sincere all the same.

The Folies-Bergère is in full swing. Marlon gazes at the pretty barmaid, an innocent in a wilderness of iniquity. It is Alice. In the mirror behind her, he sees an older man, with a beard and in a dark hat – a mysterious figure ghosting into the scene, but not featuring in the foreground. It is himself. He hopes the authorities will be gracious, and publicly acknowledge his bequest in good faith. There was little else The Great Splonjini would ever be noted for.

End.

Art References: Édouard Manet (1832 - 1883), *A Bar at the Folies-Bergère (1882) Courtauld Institute, London*

Vincent van Gogh (1853 - 1890), *Sunflowers series (1888) National Gallery, London; Self-Portrait with Bandaged Ear (1889) Courtauld Institute, London*

Francisco Goya (1746 - 1828), *Portrait of the Duke of Wellington (1814) National Gallery, London*

Leonardo da Vinci (1452 - 1519), *Mona Lisa, (1503) Louvre, Paris*

Last Man in Watford

"A single man leads only half a life." (Wolfgang Amadeus Mozart)

1/9

Margaret, known to her numerous friends as Mog, regarded herself as one of life's loners. Having regular friends and being a loner can, of course, seem incongruous, but Margaret had made up her mind.

Heading into her late twenties, childless and without a partner, she was resigned to a continuation of the same-old lifestyle, mundane clerical job, appreciation of the arts, and in particular, a love of classical music – not a CV to set a dating agency ablaze with enquiries from hot males. Not that she craved the attention of hot males anyway.

She was tall and slim, and certainly not unattractive, though she was conscious of her slightly hooked nose, gappy front teeth, and a natural tendency for her breasts to point outwards a tad when unsupported. She had experienced several boyfriends over the years, although she could not justifiably be labelled promiscuous. In no single affair, however, could she have contemplated a long-term live-in relationship. In a nutshell, she found guys at the office dull, and single men into art or classical music, like herself, lacking personality. And, of course, like-poles repel each other. Stalemate.

Her dilemma was not eased by her sense of social ineptitude, albeit a view not shared by anyone who knew her, and who generally warmed to her fatalistic philosophy and funny self-deprecation.

The odd 'girls night out' seldom threw up any realistic prospects, whereas others in her circle would 'score' on a regular basis, and probably spend the rest of the week keeping everyone informed of progress and gossip, juicy or otherwise. But then, Mog never glossed her lips, nor wore hemlines or heels too high. She simply wasn't interested in attracting male attention in that way. Her friends would light-heartedly tease her, and a standing joke was that as soon as Mog bought herself a decent pair of fuck-me shoes, marital bliss would inevitably follow.

Another negative which niggled her was feeling ill-at-ease with kids, never knowing quite how to relate to them and their media-driven lives, given the adult staidness of her own. And unlike many women of her age, she didn't seem to be over-concerned that her 'body clock' was ticking down, not being consciously aware of any broodiness.

It was February in Britain – not an ideal time of the year if one is affected by depressive moods. However, Mog looked forward to a winter break relaxing at home, in the warm, with her TV and her symphonies. Many of her friends were going off skiing in the Spanish Pyrenees. Mog knew only too well it would involve a lot of drinking, a lot of falling over, and probably a lot of ill-advised sex with swarthy Catalonian ski instructors called José. The others had tried, in vain, to cajole her into coming. Mog responded with absolute and unwaivable conviction, insisting she would rather have hot coals inserted into places where the sun didn't shine than be sat with twisted body parts, in freezing snow, on a foreign mountain.

Several days later, she recalled those exact sentiments as she sat on the cold, wet seat of the dual gondola transporting her and an unknown Frenchman's halitosis up to the intermediate lift station, to enrol in the beginners ski class.

2/9

Through his innovative concert tours, combining classical and contemporary music, Paul Duval had become well-known in the entertainment industry. His latest venture, "The World in Music", a series filmed for TV, had catapulted him to celebrity status.

Shot in unique locations, each show would typically see him interviewing, or performing with, accomplished singers and musicians. His looks and charisma enabled good chemistry to bubble between himself and female guests, appealing to both the prime-time viewing public and musical purists. Although modestly claiming not to be concert pianist standard, his mastery of the piano and knowledge of music in all its forms, earned him huge respect.

His personal life had taken a dive a couple of years previously, losing his wife to cancer. She had been his one true love, and the mother of their child Elizabeth. For a while he had struggled to cope, but found solace by immersing himself in his work and travel. But he was concerned that his daughter lacked a mother-figure, and he was torn between his exciting lifestyle and a duty to remarry.

He had employed a series of nannies, and they managed, of sorts. Often they even accompanied Paul and the TV crew to various locations in Europe and America, with Elizabeth playing cameo roles in some of his programmes, being at the televisually cute age she was. In the end, Paul decided to enter her at a top Sussex boarding school. It was the hardest day of his life when he deposited her for her first term, and for the time being bade her farewell. He drove away, pulling in at the first convenient spot, and wept uncontrollably.

He had told Elizabeth that he would telephone every evening, and if she was the slightest bit unhappy, he would come immediately and pull her out. At the end of the first week, he rang as normal. "Daddy, you don't have to keep calling every night, you know. We're having a pyjama party in Nicola's room, and I'll be missing it if we talk too much. I'll ring you if I have any problems. Bye bye, love you." He was rarely put in his place, but this time he put the phone down, shaken. He was relieved that she was happy, but somehow sad at the same time. It was as if he'd lost her.

3/9

Mog was already beginning to rue her decision to fill in for someone who'd had to drop out just prior to the holiday. Good nature had got the better of her, faced with the prospect that her friend's pre-paid holiday money would otherwise go down the tubes. Approaching the top station, she now realised her goggles would not fit over her glasses, and without her glasses, life was a blur. But then, "What's new?" she thought to herself.

Then there was the innocent sound of carbon fibre on carbon fibre, and two seconds later, one of her ill-secured skis had slid out of the cage and was plummeting to the depths of the ravine over which the gondola was passing. There was much shouting and laughing from a noisy party of young schoolgirls in the chairs behind. Mog looked for support towards her random French travelling companion. The only sympathy she could summon was a Gallic shrug. At the top, she made straight for the storage cabin.

"No tengo reemplazo para su tipo." The local jobsworth told Mog he didn't have any skis suitable for her. She tried to convince him, in her best Spanish, that she needed just to borrow a set of skis to get her through her first morning. She would be able to return them as soon as she got herself sorted out back down at the shop, where she had hired the doomed originals. "No tengo reemplazo," was his final unhelpful word, accompanied by a gesture demonstrating Gallic shrugs were not the exclusive domain of the French.

"Paco," a man's voice intruded. "Hablemos, por favor."

Moments later, Mog had a replacement pair. They needed adjusting, then she would be in time for lesson one. "How on earth did you manage that?" she demanded, quite annoyed that his short intervention had produced a result where her own carefully crafted requests had yielded nothing.

"I've been here before," replied the blurred man with an oddly familiar voice. "You have to get the inflection just right up here in the mountains, and there's a bit of Catalan about it too. Anyway, see how you get on with these."

Mog knew she should have been really thankful, but she still bristled with indignation at the thought she had been fobbed off because she was a mere woman, and couldn't possibly be expected to speak the lingo.

By mid-afternoon, the beginners class had slipped, slid and fallen headlong down the nursery slopes countless times, practising how to snow plough stop and turn, and were tentatively traversing the bottom section of the green run, heading down to the chair lift back to the hotel. Most were ready for a drink and a spot of late lunch. Mog was ready for the plane home.

"How could anyone find this remotely enjoyable?" she protested to herself. And as if to emphasise her point, she fell over again, attempting a stem turn.

A junior set of skis swished broadside across her and brought their wearer to an abrupt halt. The little girl examined Mog intently. Mog would normally have said, "Bugger off," but was past caring.

"Hello. My name's Lizzie."

'Is it?' thought Mog. 'Well, good for you.' The last thing she wanted was a spoilt brat making fun of her. Relenting her hard line, Mog answered civilly, "Would that be Elizabeth, then?"

"Yes," replied the girl. "Daddy calls me Elizabeth when he's cross with me. But most of the time he calls me Lizzie." Then she beamed. "What's yours?"

"I'm Margaret," Mog reluctantly admitted, before uncharacteristically opening up. "People call me Mog, even when they ARE cross with me, which is most of the time."

Lizzie grinned. "You lost your ski this morning. We saw it drop. My daddy's name is Paul. He's ever so clever. I have to go now. Cheerio."

"Bye..." Mog said, watching as the brat sped off effortlessly to catch up her classmates.

As Mog stared forlornly at her ski boots, wondering how she was going to get through another nine days of this, the blurred man with the oddly familiar voice glided to a halt beside her. "How are you getting on with those skis?" he enquired.

Mog considered that her ungainly seated pose, one ski attached, one detached, with snow over her jacket, and bobble-hat at an angle, should have provided enough visual evidence on its own to satisfy his query. But, for politeness, and through gratitude for his earlier assistance, she replied: "They keep coming off. And the more they come off, the wetter my arse is getting."

"Oh dear," he said. "Let's have a look at the bindings, perhaps they're too slack. It's best not to have them too tight though – the ski is supposed to detach when you fall, that's what stops you breaking a leg." He tweaked the screw adjustments. "There, see how that feels."

"Thank you, but please don't waste time on me – looks like you've got your work cut out already with that lot," Mog remarked, nodding towards the school group who were now out of sight down the slope.

"Oh, it's OK," he reassured her. "I'm on rearguard patrol duty. As long as they stick to the piste, I can mop up any stragglers. Was that Lizzie you were talking to?"

"Yes. I don't think she could understand how anyone could be as incompetent as me."

He smiled. "Oh, I'm sorry. She does rabbit a bit. I hope she didn't bend your ear too much. I'll make sure you get down, they'll be closing the runs soon. There's just a steepish bit over this brow where you need to make a couple of turns, then you can shush down to the lift station."

"Shush?" thought Mog. "Shush? What planet was this alien from?"

4/9

A wet, cold, bruised, aching and embarrassed Mog checked in her skis and boots at the hire shop, and joined the queue for the dual-chair lift final descent to the hotel, finding herself behind the bevy of noisy schoolgirls. The one called Elizabeth was in-line to board the next chair, the 'rearguard patrol' teacher with the oddly familiar voice in accompaniment. But, much against the rules, and to the vocal chagrin of the Spanish lift attendant, the 'niña estúpida' suddenly bolted forward and jumped alongside her two friends who occupied the chair already departed.

Rearguard patrolman was not amused. "Elizabeth!!" he called out, uselessly. He turned to Mog, shook his head and sighed. "That girl... sorry... do you mind if I share a ride with you?"

Mog wasn't feeling particularly sociable, but had no reason to object.

The rarefied atmosphere of the mountains, away from man-made noise pollution and with no control over one's mode of transportation, made an ideal environment in which to converse. They exchanged appreciative comment about the starkly beautiful scenery over which they floated, with the sun now low in the south west making the tops of snowy ridges glisten as though encrusted with diamonds, in contrast to the gloom of the rapidly darkening glades. The man pointed to some distant peaks. "That's Andorra. Used to be a smuggler's paradise before Spain and France both became EU. They say life expectancy there is higher than anywhere else in the world. Closest you can get to El Dorado."

"Perish the thought," Mog said, unimpressed by the idea for living forever.

"Cheer up," the man said. "You'll feel better by the end of the week. First day or two is always a trial when you're learning. They do a wonderful 'chocolate caliente con ron' – that's hot chocolate with rum, in the apres ski bar. Warms you up a treat."

"Hmm," Mog said, slightly miffed he considered it necessary to translate something so elementary for her benefit, and thinking more in terms of heading straight to her room for a hot bath. "You're one of the teachers, I presume?"

"It's a girls boarding school. I'm not on the staff, although I do sometimes help out. I'm a 'volunteer parent'. They sometimes want extra male 'protective influence', as they put it. In reality, they need someone to lug the baggage on and off the buses."

Mog smiled. "So... Elizabeth? Is that your daughter?"

"Motor-mouth? Yes."

Mog imagined that perhaps he'd packed her off to school for some peace and quiet, but didn't suggest so. She also wondered where the mother was, but thought better not to be nosy.

5/9

"Where have you been?" Mog's friends teased her. "We were going to send out a search party."

Everyone was sitting around in the bar, enjoying a well-earned rest, and noisily recounting the day's adventures. Some were already on their second or third drink, and the mood was getting increasingly cheery.

"My skis kept coming off," complained Mog. "I had to be helped down the mountain." They laughed good-naturedly. Mog was used to it.

"So you haven't pulled yet?" someone chirped, and they all laughed again.

The school group was assembling in a sectioned-off area of the restaurant, and people were at the bar organising refreshments for them. The blurred man with the oddly familiar voice started to walk towards the bay occupied by Mog's merry band. Suddenly, there was deathly quiet, and girls were nudging each other and pointing with hands under the table. Mouths were dropping open.

"What?" enquired Mog, oblivious to whatever was occurring.

More pointing. More nudging.

"Eh?" said Mog, at a loss without her specs.

"Paul Duval – off the telly...", "Daily Mail's most eligible bachelor...", "The thinking woman's crumpet...", "Sexiest man on the planet...", were some of the excitedly whispered accolades.

Paul arrived at the table and delivered a large, steaming glass mug of hot chocolate for Mog. "Chocolate caliente, con ron doble – that's with double rum!"

'He did it again – why the translation?' thought Mog. But it looked and smelt good. "Muchas gracias señor," she graciously thanked him.

"Nada – you're welcome," he said with a charming smile, and walked back to his duties.

Mog's gobsmacked companions stared at her, open mouthed... and green with envy.

"Oh, Paul Duval... yes, I thought he sounded

familiar. I didn't have my glasses on," Mog said matter-of-factly.

"And...?" they all said in unison.

"We skied together... shared a chair lift, actually." Mog tried to maintain her customary cool and humility, but it was difficult. She felt silly not having recognised one of the few men in the world she would readily give herself to, but at the same time, now guiltily enjoyed being the centre of attention, as someone with exclusive access to an international sex-symbol. But she was already thinking ahead too. Could this be the start of something? Something very special indeed.

6/9

Paul and Mog's paths didn't cross for a couple of days. The school party had gone off to Formigal, to explore, shop, and do some ice-skating. Meanwhile, a boisterous group of footballers had arrived, and were making their presence felt both on the slopes and in the hotel. A couple of them were first-time skiers, and had joined the beginners class in which Mog was gradually getting more proficient and staying upright for longer. They were a bit of a nuisance, slowing down the group, but Mog found it reassuring there was someone even worse than she was on her first day.

His name was Gary. Unlike Mog, he just laughed his head off each time he fell. It was difficult to see him ever getting the hang of it – whatever the instructor said, Gary seemed intent on doing the opposite. But he amused the whole class, and one couldn't help warming to him. Except Mog. Her problem was that this clumsy buffoon had somehow latched onto her, as though she was some kind of expert, eager to be consulted. "You're so graceful, your parallel turns... how do you get that good?" he would say.

'How did I get saddled with you?' she would think. Mog couldn't even shake off his attentions in the apres ski hours. Somehow he always would be close-by in the bar, noisily joking with his mates, and plying Mog with drinks at every opportunity. The footballers certainly livened things up, mixing well with Mog's friends, the one called Mark hitting it off especially well with Mog's room-mate Emma.

Saturday was the hotel's fancy dress night. Everyone made an effort, and it was really good fun. Mog managed to borrow a traditional Spanish costume dress, bright red, strapless, with ruched skirt, from one of the hotel staff. Some oversized ear-rings and hair pinned back, and instantly she was the Flamenco Dancing Queen. Despite the tedium of never-ending jokes about her maracas, Mog managed to enjoy herself, even if she did sup a sangria or two too many, and end up dancing round Gary who was dressed approximately as Elvis. Feeling a little woosie, she headed off to her room.

After entering quietly, in case her room-mate was already asleep, she quickly discovered Emma not asleep at all, but with legs high in the air and being energetically humped by footballer Mark. The lovers seemed too engrossed even to notice her. She quietly said "Sowwy..." and tip-toed out of the room, leaving them to it.

This was rather inconvenient, not to say a little inconsiderate, Mog thought. She headed back to the lounge where she decided to sit and wait for half an hour or so. Stuck into a 'Places to go, things to do in Zaragoza' brochure, she wasn't aware that company had arrived.

"Hello again," a familiar-sounding voice said. It was Paul, finally back from the school excursions. "Bizet's Carmen, I presume?"

Mog's heart fluttered. She was momentarily lost for words, but recovered sufficiently quickly to swing her plan into action. "Margaret, actually," she replied. "Generic flamenco dancer."

"Very good," he complimented her. "But you're a bit off the beaten track in these parts. Flamenco is much more popular in the south."

"Yes, I know," said Mog. "It's just a bit of fun for the fancy dress night." Mog realised she needed to work on his annoyingly patronising attitude – he obviously wasn't aware that she was as well versed in musical matters as anybody. "To be honest, I prefer the classical style of Spanish guitar, as pioneered by Andrés Segovia, for instance, rather than the percussive sounds of flamenco."

"Me too," Paul replied, encouragingly. "I love Rodrigo's Recuerdos de la Alhambra. They let me do some filming at the Palace there. Wonderful location."

"Tárrega, you mean," said Mog, imagining she would score points for correcting him about the composer.

"No, I think you'll find it was Rodrigo, but it doesn't matter. Look, I've been meaning to ask you..."

Mog knew damn well she was right, but turned her boiling blood down to 'simmer' on hearing his 'ask you'. 'Oh my word! Ask me what?' she wondered.

"It's just that from time to time, school holidays especially, or while I'm working out of the country... and Lizzie does seem to have taken a shine to you... I was wondering..."

'Wondering what? Wondering what?' Mog

herself was wondering, her heart racing.

"I do need... well..."

'Need what? Need what?' Mog was silently living her wildest dreams.

"I have to get another nanny for Elizabeth. You do seem to fit the bill, so, if you popped your CV over to my office, we could perhaps come to some arrangement. Anyway, I'll leave it with you. Let me know later what you think. I need to go now and check back in."

And Mog was left sitting alone, staring through a transparent Zaragoza tourist brochure at an image of her bleak, loveless future. She was too stunned even for tears.

7/9

"What's up, doll? I can't bear to see you looking so sad." It was Elvis, more than a little worse for wear.

"Go away, Gary," Mog replied, knowing she would need to say it several times before it registered with him.

Gary sat beside her on the lounger. "I was off to bed, but Mark's got the room key and I can't find him anywhere. You sure you're OK, doll?"

Mog knew exactly where Mark was, but didn't let on. In no way did she want to give Gary any ideas. "Gary, you're totally stocious."

"Oh babe," Gary slurred, "You're such a turn on when you use those lovely words. But honest, I don't deserve them – I'm not really that special. I'm just an ordinary guy..."

"It means you're drunk, you idiot."

"No, no!" Gary protested. "Just tired – hard skiing, the mountain air, a couple of San Miguels, untox-hicated by the sweet perfume of the fabulous fatal femme Mog with the Mog-nificent maracas..."

And within seconds his doe eyes were shut and slumber had overtaken him. His head flopped onto her bare shoulder, leaving her to contemplate her hopeless situation. It seemed the chances of her winning the affections of the suave, talented and successful aesthete Paul were as remote as those of good-natured but thick-skinned and uncultured Gary ever getting anywhere with her. She carefully laid Gary's head on the armrest of the settee, and set off again for her own room, where happily, her room-mate Emma was asleep, alone.

8/9

It was the last day on the slopes. Everyone agreed it had been a great holiday. Even Mog, who eventually had become quite a stylish skier, had to admit it was sad they all soon would be going home, maybe because right now, the sanctuary and solitude of her own home seemed less inviting than it usually was.

On the final run, guys and gals were confidently showing off their new-learnt skills, taking liberties with tight turns, and audaciously jumping over enticing brows. Then disaster.

Emma skied recklessly across Mog, who almost went flying trying to avoid a collision. But Emma lost it altogether and fell heavily, crumpling in a heap, and emitting alarming moans and groans. Mog rushed to her aid.

"I've done my shoulder, Mog," Emma croaked. "Oooh..."

Mog was no first-aider. "Don't try to move," was all she could think to say. Her friend's obvious distress was painful to witness, and not knowing exactly what to do heightened Mog's state of panic. Some of the others started to arrive, including Gary, who came to an ugly halt with his customary flop-dive.

With an uncharacteristic air of authority, Gary rushed over to where Emma lay. "Whoa, Emm, this is no time for an afternoon nap," he joked. "Let's have a look-see what you've been and done."

"Rubbing liniment on a bruised shin doesn't make one a paramedic, Gary," Mog said. "We must get her to hospital."

Gary carried on regardless. "Looks like a slight dislocation. We may be in luck. The more we do now, the better the chances of good recovery. The longer we leave it, you'll end up needing a general anaesthetic – you'll be out of action for ages...

"Jeff, ski down to the lift station, get them to radio for the mountain rescue – they can stretcher her down. Get them to arrange an ambulance from town – whatever we do now, we'll want it checked out and X-rayed...

"RICE – that's what we want. Not paella, though. Rest, Ice, Compression, Elevation...

"Here," taking off his ski-jacket, "someone stuff this full of snow. I'll do a cold-pack sling, wrap it tight for compression and tie the sleeves to support the arm... it might even pop back into place naturally after this...

"Check pulse... regular... strong... hey Emm, good news, you're still alive. Let's try a little reduction... gentle rotation... scream if it hurts..."

Mog watched incredulously. Was this 'her' Gary, a man on a mission competently taking charge like George Clooney in ER? What if he made things worse?

Mark sensed Mog's anxiety about Gary's proficiency, and quietly reassured her that his roomie was training to be a physio, which surprised but relieved her somewhat.Then came the answer to the second question. Emma groaned, groaned again, then uttered "Aaah... that's so much better." It seemed as if the ball-joint had indeed 'popped back in'.

The rescue team arrived impressively quickly. They were complimentary about Gary's handling of the incident, and their sled, laden with Emma, with Mark in attendance, soon disappeared down the slopes to rendezvous with the waiting ambulance.

Mog couldn't help herself but wrap her arms round Gary and plant on him probably the biggest sloppy kiss he'd ever had. "I am SO proud of you," she admitted.

9/9

Mog had been a singleton in the morning chair lift ascent. She had been able to reflect on her love-life in idyllic silence. Now, on the final descent, after spending the previous week trying to avoid Gary, she happily rode down with him, brimming with admiration.

"How long have you been training to be a physio?" she asked casually.

"Oh, about a week or so," Gary answered.

Mog couldn't help smiling. A week or so? It restored her faith in his irrepressible resilience.

"That's Andorra over there," Mog indicated. "They say life expectancy there is higher than anywhere else in the world. Closest you can get to El Dorado."

"Really? Fascinating," said Gary, impressed with her knowledge. "What a thought, eh? Mind you, it would depend on who you were shacked up with for those never-ending years..." And with his doe-eyes he looked lovingly at Mog, who, recalling her own earlier less positive opinions about immortality, raised her eyebrows in dismissal of his incorrigible optimism.

"Um... talking about shacking up..." Gary continued, tentatively.

Mog quickly interjected. "Gary, I wouldn't shack up with anyone who thought Andrés Segovia was someone who played football for Real Madrid. Not even if he was the last man in Watford."

After a few moments came Gary's inevitable response. "So that's a maybe, then?"

Mog realised that being a loner with good friends was what she was comfortable with. Always competing, or constantly having to adapt, to make a relationship work, was never going to make for a happy life. Here was an opportunity to carry on being the same person she was, but with a ready-made supply of love and support from a capable, funny, attractive man who was impervious to her dismissive sarcasm and negativity.

Realising she would otherwise miss Gary more than her poor heart could stand, Mog snuggled up to him, her head on his shoulder, a hand on his chest, and purred encouragingly, "Maybe..."

End.

The Well-Read American

Jack stumbles for real into some classic works of literature, with results he didn't bargain for!

1/9

Jack Durvill was an accomplished professor of literature at the Missouri State University. Along with holding regular student tutorials in creative writing and appreciation, he often fulfilled guest-speaking roles at national symposia, and would supply publishers with critiques of authors and novels, for forewords and fly-covers of new print runs, and the like. Un-professorially outgoing and popular, Jack was as familiar with English classic 'favourites' like Dickens and the Brontës, as he was with more contemporary American 'favorites' like Steinbeck and Hemingway.

He had recently reached 'the big 40' years of age. His one failed marriage had ended in divorce several years earlier. Away from reading, writing and lecturing, only one pastime currently came close to competing with his pursuit of busty fun-loving female post-grads, and that was researching his genealogy.

So, he decided on a celebratory vacation in

England. This would enable him to seek out his roots, and experience at first-hand its unique locations, to appreciate better what had inspired great writers to set their stories there. Jack had been once before to Britain, for a literary conference in London. On that occasion he ventured no further than the city limits, exploring the popular tourist hot-spots, Dickensian back-streets, museums and libraries, and a municipal building called Somerset House, where one can trace one's family history.

His grandfather had maintained that the American Durvills originated as French colonists in the 17th century. But Somerset House and The British Library had indicated to the contrary, and that a similarly named family had held a seat in the West Country of England a good century later, but relinquished it following some sort of scandal.

2/9

Jack's flight duly arrived at Heathrow. Being in the frame of mind he was, he decided he would rename the airport Heathcliff, with obvious associations with the Wuthering Heights that a Boeing 787 could achieve. His excitement overcame any jet-lag, and he immediately hired a car to transport himself via the Cotswolds and Shakespeare's Stratford-on-

Avon, to Somerset and Jane Austen's dwelling in Bath, to Dorset for Thomas Hardy's Wessex, and on to Devon, and Dartmoor – that beautiful, but brooding, eerie expanse with its notorious prison, and of course, Conan Doyle's setting for his most famous Sherlock Holmes mystery.

By the fourth day, Jack had got the hang of driving on the wrong side of the road, and of making himself understood, having initially believed, mistakenly, that everybody spoke the same mother tongue. To compound communication problems, dialects changed as he moved through one county to the next. But he was loving every minute, despite the quirky customs and unavailability of decent steaks or bourbon. He finally arrived at his Devon destination, where he was cordially welcomed at 'Ye Old Stump Inn', a lodging house in the unremarkable village of Fondleham-by-the-Brook, which lay between Bovey Tracey and Widecombe-in-the-Moor.

His genial hosts, the Glumms, Fred and Marge, showed him to their very best room. He suspected it was the only room, but no matter. The Park Lane Hilton it was not. But then, the Park Lane Hilton didn't have characterful low beams on which one could merrily crack one's skull, creaky floorboards the noise of which would waken the dead, or an atmosphere so thick with history and mystery one needed to swim one's way through it to reach the bathroom which was way along the passage. After just one night, Jack decided he needed to go easy on the local Devon cider, if only to minimise the number of nocturnal trips down the corridor.

3/9

He mapped out his first full day on the moor, and after a hearty Glumm breakfast, threw his walking boots in the car, and set off, first to visit Princetown jail, then to search for the Hound of the Baskervilles. The prison museum was suitably gruesome, depicting Victorian conditions for incarcerated convicts and the barbaric violence perpetrated therein. Jack was fascinated to learn that, originally an overspill for prison-ships in the times of the Napoleonic wars, it also housed American POWs taken during the 1812 skirmishes. Few escaped from Dartmoor. In that respect, it was like Alcatraz, except that instead of being safeguarded by treacherous waters, it was surrounded by equally inhospitable moorland, with its freezing temperatures, disorientating mist, rain, bogs, sink-holes and wild creatures.

To the average holidaymaker, things would be looking grim, but Jack could only revel in the living atmosphere of the whole area, reasoning that whereas some locations were photogenic, others could be equally literagenic, if that was a word – he'd have to check, lending themselves readily to fictional fantasy. He drove back across the moor, and located the craggy hillock named Hound Tor, reportedly the site where the Baskerville legend originated.

On trudging back down from the Tor summit to the car park, where he and several other tourists had left their vehicles, he was reminded of the ever-resilient British sense-of-humour. A mobile café had arrived, serving hot food and drink to grateful hikers. Jack smiled wryly at the garish sign-writing on the side of the van, announcing its identity: 'The Hound of the Basket Meals'. He wondered what Sir Arthur would have made of it.

At nearby Widecombe, merriment had been scheduled, in the form of visiting Morris dancers. To Jack's untrained eye, this consisted of men and women dressed in frilly shirts and floppy hats, wearing bells wherever bells could be worn, waving handkerchiefs, and wielding sticks dangerously. This was all done to the lively music of someone playing a squeeze-box. Every so often, sticks would engage, resulting in a loud clack. And every so often someone would fall down, either injured, or drunk. Apparently it originated as a Pagan ritual. Jack sipped his scrumpy, a locally brewed cider, at least establishing the probable cause of the endemic inebriation.

4/9

Back in Fondleham, ignoring his waistline, Jack went into Mrs Plummett's tea shop for a world-famous Devonshire Cream Tea, or so the sign claimed. (He couldn't recall it being an actual household name in St Louis, Missouri.) It comprised of a pot of tea, accompanied by scones, thick cream and jam. Delicious. As was the voluptuous Mrs Plummett, in traditional costume for the benefit of the late-season tourists.

Jack explored the rest of the quaint village, which, admittedly, didn't take much exploring. On turning back towards the inn, almost by chance, he came across the local museum. It was no more than one room in a tiny thatched cottage, housing mostly dull, rusting antique farming and household implements. Nevertheless, he wandered in for a browse. From nowhere, seemingly, a girl appeared. No surprise, she also was attired in authentic period costume, but it hung on her particularly well. She was mid-twenties, Jack guessed, and an absolute cracker.

"Tess of the D'Urbervilles?" Jack ventured, smiling, hoping to impress.

"Sire," replied the girl, feigning a blush. "How generous ye be. Alas nay. Tessie Durberfield, of whom ye speak, is from an adjacent shire, many leagues thither. Her legen'ry beauty is admired by gen'lemen an' coveted by maidens from all o'er the West Coun'ry, including myself. But please call me Tess if it amuses thee. 'Twould indeed be a sweet enjoyment."

What a find this was. It was as though he had stepped into the pages of an English classic. "Well, Tess, we do enjoy sweet things in America, you know," he said. Licking maple syrup off her breasts was actually what came foremost to mind.

"Oh, pray do tell," she implored him. "Ye be from the colonies, methinks. Tell how it is, the New World?"

Oh, how he adored the charade. And there was Tess, playing her character so perfectly, so charmingly, so alluringly. How could Thomas Hardy have treated her so mean? Jack told her where he was from, and that he was researching Conan Doyle's inspiration for the Hound mystery, as well as the origins of his own family, the Durvills.

"Of Master Doyle, I know nay," she confessed. "Ne'er a gen'leman of this parish, am I certain. But of Lord Henry D'Urville, of course, all are surely familiar."

"Please continue, sweet delightful Tess." Jack imagined she may simply be humouring him, but didn't see why he shouldn't flirt back a little.

"But the incident of Devil's Crag, sire, 'tis well documented." She led him past the minefield of museum pieces spread about the floor, and pointed out the old manuscripts, newspaper cuttings and maps displayed on the rear wall.

Jack's loins stirred as she brushed past him, the linen of her chemise against his arm, the crinoline of her full skirt against his leg. Her demeanour, her purity – surely an angel sent to brighten his day. His life, maybe. One could wish, but right now he needed to concentrate. He read avidly the article from a time-yellowed page of the Tavistock Clarion, realising very quickly this was exactly where Conan Doyle had poached the Baskerville legend, which in essence was:

'...young pretty serving wench abducted by debauched drunken hunting party... escapes their lustful clutches by fleeing across the moor at night... pursued by the said mounted huntsmen, with pack of hounds trained with her scent... the unnamed woman never seen again... Lord Henry found dead on Devil's Crag, horror-struck expression etched on his face... reports of a monstrous hound of Hell...'

The girl waited until Jack had digested the text, then quickly added: "The report is confused, sire, there be inaccuracies of some consequence. 'Twas in fact Squire Pidgen, the wicked master of the hunt who perished, at the hand of the noble Lord Henry, who gallan'ly strove in vain to save the maiden's life. This good Henry D'Urville then fled into exile to avoid the gallows. Rumour has't he did board a west-bound steamer at Bristol."

Jack was enthralled. He needed more time to take it all in. "Look, Tess," he apologised, "I have to get back to the inn. Mrs Glumm is doing steak and ale pie, apparently just for me. It would be so rude if I was late. Will you be here tomorrow?"

"Sire," replied the girl, as pleasantly as ever, "I am here constan'ly."

5/9

Jack tucked into Marge Glumm's pie. It was worth crossing the Atlantic for. He related his day's adventures to her and Fred, who were only too delighted to be catering for such an unusual and colourful visitor. When he mentioned the episode in the museum, they listened intently, but looked dubiously at each other.

"Funny," Fred said, "museum's not been open all season. We 'ad the 'ealth and safety people in from Tavistock – was a major fire 'azard, risk to public life 'n limb they said, oo-arr."

Jack shrugged. Well, at least Jack knew one

thing the locals didn't. He did agree it was a fire-trap though. Remembering his resolution, he limited his evening nightcap to just one glass of 'Stump Inn Special', and bade goodnight to his hosts.

Judiciously calling by the bathroom first, Jack finally reached his room, where his comfortable bed beckoned. The events of the day were swimming through his brain, especially the museum experience. As he began unbuttoning his shirt, he suddenly became aware that he was not alone. He wheeled round, startled. But fright turned to delight. Pure joy, in fact. It was Tess from the cottage. Dressed just as she was earlier. Looking every bit as irresistible as before, with shining hazel eyes and a loving smile that would melt Alaska.

"But my Lord Henry," she purred, "my sweetest redeemer, thou who hast captured my heart for eternity, allow a lowly peasant maiden to assist in thy task."

On very few occasions was Jack lost for words, but this was one of them. She approached him, and finished unbuttoning his shirt. She gently tugged the tails out of his jeans and caressed his bare upper body with hands so warm and soft his knees trembled and he thought he would crumple. Again, the material of her chemise had a magical effect on him, brushing tantalizingly against his wide chest.

Jack was consciously aware that he should have been thinking 'Who is this girl who suddenly has popped up so brazenly in my bedroom?', 'Am I being set-up for some ruinous scam?', 'Am I taking advantage of someone who is vulnerable?', 'Should I be thinking in terms of taking precautions?'. Yes, he knew that's what he should have been thinking. But he was helpless, as though trapped in some kind of psychokinetic time warp, and had never ever felt this way before.

As she continued to undress him, he peered down her halter-neck top at lily-white flesh leading to soft curves of young breasts, imagining that they'd never been touched. As his jeans fell to the floor, and she eased down his shorts, he tried to hide his acute embarrassment by shutting his weary eyes, though her thin cotton skirt flicked against his legs, arousing him even further. He decided bizarrely that kissing her would somehow reduce his self-consciousness, so he held her shoulders and brushed his mouth over the side of her neck. She tossed back her head, gasping, inviting his lips to her bosom, and onwards towards her pulsating heart.

Finally, she pushed him gently backwards, and he fell upon the bed. And as he lay there, entranced, she pulled at some tie-strings, and one by one, each part of her costume slithered from her silken body onto the bedroom floor...

He couldn't remember eventually falling asleep, but fall asleep he obviously had done, and it was breakfast time before he came to. The rest had done him good, and he felt refreshed. But seconds later, everything rushed back to him. He realised he was alone. The beautiful, enigmatic Tess, like an exotic bird of paradise, had flown.

6/9

Over breakfast, Jack thought it imprudent to mention the girl in his room. However, he was desperate to meet up with her again, so he rather bolted Mrs Glumm's 'full English cholesterol-buster', in order to make an early start.

"Any plans for th'day, Professor Durvill?" asked Fred. "I's afraid old forecast's not so hot, oo-arr. Be stayin' off th'moor if I wuz you."

"We have some pretty scary tornadoes back in Missouri," said Jack, playing down Fred's concern. "Guess we know how to handle a bit of English breeze."

Fred shrugged, sincerely hoping his valued customer wouldn't live to regret his bravado.

Once away from the inn, Jack made straight for the cottage museum. To his dismay, it was closed. Checking the notice in the door, which implied it was closed until further notice, he was startled to spot the map, which had hung next to the newspaper cutting the previous day, but was now prominent above the 'closed' sign. And close to Devil's Crag someone had pencilled a cross. What could be the significance? Only one way to find out, resolved Jack.

He strode back to the inn for his car, passing, as he did so, the Reverend Blunt outside the little church, updating the woefully low steeple restoration appeal fund thermometer. "Good morning," the man of cloth cheerfully greeted him.

Of course. The vicar will know every damn body and thing that's going on around here. Sure he'll know Tess and where she is. Jack related his story, watering down the section not suitable for ecclesiastical consumption.

"Hmm," pondered the reverend, rubbing his chin. "Well, dear boy, our museum's definitely been closed all year. And as for Fondleham's flock being blessed with its own Tess of the D'Urbervilles impersonator... er, the good landlord Glumm hasn't been plying you with that evil scrumpy of his, has he?"

It wasn't the answer Jack wanted to hear. "Never mind," he said, "I'm off to take a look at Devil's Crag."

"Oh dear." The vicar seemed alarmed. "I

wouldn't do that if I were you, dear boy, they say the Good Lord is blowing a storm in from the west to quench our thirsty lands, Tavistock is awash..."

But Jack was already marching on. "Thanks, Reverend, see you later."

7/9

Jack was getting to know his way around, and managed to hit on the narrow track from the main Buckland-over-Moor road, leading him close to Devil's Crag. He parked up, and set foot to where he figured the pencilled cross must have marked. The air had taken on an autumnal feel and the strengthening wind added to the chill factor. Jack wished he'd put on extra clothing, but it was too late now.

He was nearing the top of the crag, and he was getting out of puff. He had also worked up a sweat, and its rapid evaporation was causing him to shiver. The threatening skies and worsening visibility began to merge the terrain of rocky outcrop, gorse and heather into one dark grey mass. Nothing significant here was going to be discernible, so Jack decided to beat a retreat. That's when Tess appeared, a few dozen yards in front of him, beckoning him on, like a shining beacon.

She was dressed as normal, in her light summer blouse and frock. She was calm and smiling, as usual. How could she appear so, out here in such adverse weather conditions? Jack had no choice. He hurried to reach her.

He rounded the last large cragstone before the summit. She must be waiting here. But no. There was nothing. Nothing, except a pile of small-to-medium boulders. Jack took hold of the top one, intending to hurl it down the hill in angry frustration. It was heavier than he bargained for. He managed to topple it from the apex of the pile, and in doing so, dislodged another stone further down. There, exposed, was that a bone? The carcass of some animal - a sheep maybe?

As another rock shifted, a huge black storm cloud materialised directly overhead, reducing the area to darkness. Jack looked skywards. By a freak of nature, the cloud assumed the dreadful shape of the head of a snarling hound with menacing red eyes. A strong gust whipped up around the crag, and a vicious fork of lightning lit up both the rocks, and the human skull which had rolled out, freed from the weight of boulders which had incarcerated it for heaven-only knows how long. An ear-splitting thunderclap was followed by torrential hail.

Jack's 40-year-old legs couldn't carry him fast enough down the hill to where his car stood. In blind panic he had slipped and fallen several times, grazing knees   and elbows, and scratching himself to pieces on the prickly gorse. Miraculously he found the car, and sat in the driving seat, panting, shivering, bleeding, soaking wet and covered in mud.

Too many things had happened simultaneously for Jack's nervous system to cope with, not to mention his sense of reasoning. Had he been magically lured to this place to pay some retribution for sins of a forefather? Where was the girl, was she out there, or had she found shelter? What was she doing out here anyway? And whose was the skeleton?

Too many unknowns. Jack needed help. After regaining some composure, he decided to risk driving back along the ill-defined track, to the nearest place he could pick up a cell-phone signal, and call the emergency number.

Police and rescue services came promptly to meet him. They were less than impressed that some dumb-ass tourist had ambled out onto the moors in this weather. However, they were interested in the mention of human remains.

8/9

Jack extended his vacation. He had provided statements for the authorities, but wanted to stay until the various forensic examinations were complete, and he could attain some sort of closure. It turned out that the skeleton was that of a young woman. It was hard to date, but reckoned to be anything up to a couple of hundred years old. Jack went to see Reverend Blunt.

"A Christian burial? Oh no, dear boy, out of the question. Far too many difficulties - matters of jurisdiction, rights of ownership of the remains, agreement from the Diocesan Advisory Council, and so on and so forth..."

"I noticed that your 'Save the Steeple Fund' is well short of its target," Jack said, changing the subject. "It would be such a shame if it toppled down before you   could scrape the money together... I was wondering... a small donation maybe... just a modest few thousand dollars, perhaps..."

"Oh dear boy!" Reverend Blunt's eyes rolled like cash registers. "God moves in such mysterious ways, His wonders to perform... a burial you say, dear boy? I'll see what I can do."

9/9

None of the few attendees could really understand why the American was so emotional. But then, the solemnity of such occasions often had a similar effect on the most rational of people. Jack watched as the ushers, one by one, threw handfuls of soil into the tiny grave. For some reason, Jack lifted his head, possibly because someone in brighter apparel had caught the corner of his eye. He froze.

Not thirty paces away stood Tess, as ever, looking radiant, in that same simple costume. Her smile flashed at Jack across the graveyard, and raising a hand, she gestured a secret lover's farewell.

Jack grabbed the landlord's arm, pointing towards where Tess stood. Fred, relatively unmoved by the whole occasion, remained so, shaking his head in polite incomprehension. Jack looked again towards the spot, but no longer was she there.

"...ashes to ashes, dust to dust..." the reverend droned, nearing the finish of the service.

Jack bent down, and added his own handful of soil, whispering his own parting words to the young woman he now knew he would never see again. "Tess... my brave English rose, my love for eternity... at last, rest in peace."

End.

Nude Reclining

A budding French artist and his unlikely BBW model.

1/1

Raymond DuCroix (b.1825 Chamonix, France) was one of the father figures of the French Impressionist movement in the mid 19th century.

Talented though he was, much of his early work involving the female form was mocked by savvy critics of the day because of the inaccuracies in some of the anatomical detail. Hard to believe in this day and age that an adult man could be so ignorant of what lay beneath a woman's bodice and petticoat. But even Renoir, possibly the most famous impressionist of them all, was not confident about depicting female nudity until after developing an intimate relationship with Lise Tréhot, who subsequently modelled for him.

The youthful and gauche DuCroix was not city bred, and arrived in the capital from a mountain region of France. He had hitherto never been with a girl, and this was quite obvious from his early nude paintings showing women with manly pecs on flat chests, upturned soup bowl breasts with petit-pois nipples, narrow hips, slim bottoms, and a laryngeal prominence.

Although he would add hair, facial details and raiment accurately, when it came to genitalia, it was all pretty much guesswork, and bad guesses at that. All this changed after a visit by DuCroix to Albert Gastonne's now famous bar on Rue de la Bête in Paris.

Gastonne's café, an artisan honeypot, was waitressed by several voluptuous and flirty girls, comely wenches of the day one might say. They often doubled, given the chance, as artist's models. And slipped a few extra francs, bed-partners too, according to rumour.

However, one of the table girls, Mlle Claudette Scallier, to whom nature had been less than kind when dishing out attributes of conventional beauty, relied entirely on a waitress's tips for her living.

On this particular evening visit, Raymond plucked up the nerve to write a message to one of the more flamboyant girls, asking that she model for a 'nude reclining' series he was undertaking. The barman delivered the note, and soon there was merriment in the bar, as the girl was heard to remonstrate loudly 'il veut me donner le con d'un buffle' (which alas does not translate politely). Suffice to say she felt her reputation for pulchritude would be compromised by her being portrayed with certain buffalo-like features. The humiliated DuCroix sat with his beer, alone and dejected.

Claudette had witnessed the incident and felt a certain empathy for the struggling artist, she too being one of society's persona non accepto. She paused by his table, glanced round to check the barman wasn't watching, then topped up his glass with beer from her jug, and swiftly moved on. DuCroix was touched by her gesture of kindness. Furthermore, after imbibing a quantity of the said ale, he had an idea. Fuelled with Dutch courage, he intercepted Mlle Scallier, and in an awkward whisper, invited her to his attic studio to model for him. And surprisingly, she readily accepted.

Her café shift over, Claudette walked the short distance to DuCroix's left bank rented room. She entered the house and climbed the several flights of stairs before very discreetly tapping on his door – a lone woman calling upon a gentleman was considered injurious to one's reputation. The artist swiftly admitted her and bade her rest in the chair, the only chair in fact, that the apartment boasted. The somewhat overweight girl was out of breath and was grateful for his consideration.

They talked banalities while each of them combatted their shyness, and DuCroix offered her a cognac in a cracked china mug. She was unused to such indulgence, and as the spirit hit the back of her throat, she coughed violently. Afraid she was choking, he patted her on the back with some force. It made no difference to the mademoiselle's digestion, but the body contact served to break the ice, and they both eventually laughed at the incident.

The couch, the only couch, awaited its reclining subject. The back drop, some tawdry screens depicting floral landscapes from Ambrosia, set the scene. "Shall I undress, monsieur?" Claudette enquired, wary that time was ticking by.

The artist's face reddened as realisation came upon him that he was about to become alone with a naked female. His painting techniques were considerable. His social skills were scant by comparison. "Perhaps behind the screen, mademoiselle," he suggested, although it seemed to matter not.

He had painted numerous portraits of women in their finery, more often than not by commission from their wealthy husbands or fathers seeking to beautify their wife or daughter for purposes of vanity, dowry or social standing. How many times had he been told to paint out that blemish or reduce that plumpness?

Mlle Scallier soon reappeared from behind the screen and presented her unclothed self. The premise that the artist/model relationship should be businesslike and objective went out the window as Raymond gazed in awe at his Claudette. "Mademoiselle is truly very beautiful," he stammered. By conventional standards she was not, but to him, she was the living Venus, only bigger.

Without a bustier corset, her voluminous unsupported breasts dropped southwards and swung as she sidled towards the divan. She was black-haired and dark-complexioned – a typically Gallic woman, and her exceptionally large areolae mesmerised and alarmed him. He never had imagined anything quite like them. She took up her reclining position. It was not exactly the pose he had in mind, but for the moment it would do.

He got to work – the unattractive facial features, her short unstyled lacklustre hair, the narrowness of her neckline, her upper arms musclebound by the constant carrying of trays of filled beer mugs. He mapped the curves of her torso and the folds of her tummy, especially noting the width of her hips, nature-designed for child-bearing. His brushes stroked the canvas with a passion, as if it were his own hands caressing her body.

He at last needed to adjust her pose. "Perhaps mademoiselle could..." and he cautiously approached her. She didn't flinch when he gently took her arm, fixing the elbow position, and then the back of her knee to complete the planned picture composition. The touch of her warm smooth skin aroused him, but he resisted, and returned to his easel.

Some while was spent meticulously blending pigments and shades to reproduce the effect of the dwindling rays of evening light which streamed through the tiny attic window, adding that vibrancy to a painting which is a principal feature of Impressionism. He hadn't noticed that Claudette had parted the mop of hair which obliterated her mons pubis, and was moving her middle finger up and down inside her vagina.

Raymond was in uncharted territory. "Mademoiselle?" was all he could think to say.

She beckoned him over. He downed his palette and approached. She reached out and offered up her moistened finger to his lips. And for the first time in his young life, he tasted a woman.

Smock and pantaloons were hurriedly discarded, and Raymond, with no previous experience to call on, fell into Claudette's open arms, simply doing what comes naturally. He discovered that deep inside her was a place not just moist, soft and warm, but animate - alive with movement, contraction and expansion, fire... and passion!

If only he could bring his paintings to life anywhere near so effectively...

"*Nude reclining #14 by Raymond DuCroix*" hangs in the Musée du Louvre on the troisième étage du Côté des Salles. The amply-proportioned woman, listed as "Claudette S", with mole on her face, twisted mouth, and a forest of unkempt black pubic hair, is holding her middle finger to her lips. There is a sheen on her enormous bosom and she has a glint in her eye... and she is looking decidedly flushed.

End.

Jane

The author throws a wobbly while paying homage to a literary icon at the British Library.

1/1

I paid a visit to the modern purpose-built British Library, which stands, or rather sprawls, next to the architecturally wondrous St Pancras Station in London.

In one of the exhibition halls, there were rows upon rows of displays of artefacts, scrolls and artwork dating back to ancient Egypt and beyond. Amongst the original parchments were musical scores by Mozart, Bach and Beethoven, complete with scrawled orchestration, blots, alterations, obliterations and smudges, such that a mediocre amateur piano player such as myself could not begin to decipher them, let alone turn them into beautiful symphonic melodies.

There too was the original parchment on which Anne Boleyn wrote, imploring Cardinal Wolsey to expedite the divorce of King Henry VIII from Catherine of Aragon, so he be free to wed his true love, namely Anne herself.

Also on display, under reinforced glass, and in subdued lighting to protect and preserve every priceless item, were sections of hand-written literary works by great English authors such as Hardy, Dickens, Carroll, Eliot and the Brontës.

I paused, as if magnetically attracted, at one particular exhibit.

It was hers. I had found it. I had arrived. The very writing desk at which she sat. A tiny, simple wood-framed workplace, complete with inkwell and blotter. There, open plainly to see, was one of her manuscripts. Not a copy, nor reproduction. *The* very pages on which she scribed her plots, inventions, commentaries and dreams. Like Beethoven's originals, it was littered with crossings-out, ringed phrases with arrows pointing to where they should be re-inserted, character name changes and spilled ink.

My knees went wobbly and I welled up. Tears fell uncontrollably from my face onto the glass plate. Fellow visitors shuffled by, anxious to cover as much of the library's collection as possible in their time available. They probably thought I was barmy.

I tried to keep my emotion in check, but continued to sob, and the glass melted away, as if dissolved by my tears ~~~~~

~~~~~ tears which directly wetted my manuscript and I became cross with myself for allowing my melancholy to damage writing paper which currently was in such scarce commodity. My brother Henry was due to visit at the weekend, should a carriage become available, and I desperately hoped he would bring a ream. A new quill pen too, if that was not too much to hope for – the nib of this one has become so troublesome.

I reviewed my morning's work. Frustrated by its untidiness, I daydreamed – shameful imaginings worthy only of a silly young girl. Henry would bring me a magic pen. One possessed of the Genie of the Dictionary. Should I carelessly misspell a word, it would, in a nonce, underscore the offending word with a squiggly line. I smiled at the ludicrousness of the idea, though it certainly would have saved my blushes as a 14-year-old on the occasion I submitted "Love and Freindship" for public approval.

My mind wandered back to the mixed fortunes of earlier in the day. My "First Impressions" effort, yet another one, rejected by the publishers, marked "Declined by return of post"... and the other strange package which the messenger claimed was already on our doorstep. It had contained a small cylinder, metallic and smooth, befitting a Maharajah's
~~~~~

jewel collection judging by its lustre and the perfection of its finish.

After luncheon, I returned to "Elinor and Marianne" wondering if the Dashwood sisters would fare better than the Bennets in the reading public's literary consciousness. Should I spice up the romantic encounters to make the work more acceptable to a male readership? After all, publishing, like everything else these days, business, politics, even the so-called electoral democracy was subject to an exclusively male stranglehold.

I recalled spice of my own. That occasion when I was but 20 years. Thomas had just graduated from university, and we came together at the September ball. I had the jolliest time of my life as we danced and danced, chatted about Oxford's marvellous Bodleian Library, and danced some more.

We wickedly sneaked a glass of Sherry, that pungent liqueur made by the over-fermentation of Spanish grapes. We also naughtily sneaked unchaperoned to outside, where the seductive moonlight teases and tempts one to make courageous and indiscreet advances on one's dancing companion. Tom leant over and kissed my lips. I remember thinking "Is that it? Is there no accompanying embrace nor awkward fondling?"

I considered swooning into his arms, but

thought better of it, having lampooned the conventions of romantic novels in my own stories. But maybe I should have, because to my surprise, he held out his hand and placed it on my breast, holding it motionless for what seemed like an eternity. An eternity which came to an abrupt end when more people noisily joined us on the patio.

Tom and I were well suited, but he was a penniless trainee barrister, and I a penniless would-be author. Such a marriage, even though sanctionable by Heaven was not socially acceptable on Earth, and we never saw each other again.

Earlier this year, some seven years on from the encounter with Tom, was my adventure with Harris. He was an unattractive man in both appearance and manner, though I myself boast not to resemble the peach placed at the top of the basket. Neither was he couth in matters of art and literature. But he was sufficient of funds and represented the safest investment for guaranteeing a degree of comfort in dotage for myself and my beloved sister Cassandra.

I accepted Harris's proposal of marriage, and that night he came to my chamber. I neither rejected his advances nor enthusiastically welcomed them. In these times, maidens are expected 'not to make a fuss' lest their name be besmirched ever more, their character being tainted whether they were willing or not.

I remember bleeding, and thinking "I am damaged goods." But I also mischievously imagined that should a future encounter occur, with a more compassionate suitor, I should be well placed, as a story teller, to explain my condition in any number of ways, like horse-riding for example, though I should be hard pressed to recount truthfully how I came to be indulging in such an exclusive recreation.

I withdrew my acceptance the following morning. A marriage devoid of affection is a life imprisonment, financial security or no.

I idly caressed the cylinder again, reminding myself of its eerily smooth, but comforting feel. To my astonishment, the receptacle started to split into two, and by twisting one half further, it opened right up.

I was somewhat disappointed. There were no new quills, and no ink bottles. And no Genie escaped from captivity, offering to reward its rescuer with untold fame and fortune. Merely a piece of card, folded as per an invitation to a ball. But alas, the writing on it made no sense.

Perhaps the sender had adopted some nom-de-plume. It was certainly a name unfamiliar to me. Indeed, the sender professed their love, which surely was mischief – I seem to socialise less and less these days. And what on earth were these 'gifts' of which they speak? I decided to postpone the puzzle until the evening, when

Cassandra would be here to assist in unravelling the mystery.

I was still fiddling with the plot lines of "Susan" when Cassie arrived. We had some tea and talked about our respective days. I broached the subject of the cylinder and the strange wording within. "Perhaps 'tis a time capsule with a message from beyond," my sister suggested playfully.

Cassandra took the card and read the message slowly and aloud. "Dearest Jane. Thank you for all your precious everlasting gifts. Much Love, Janeites everywhere."

End.

* *Jane Austen (1775 – 1817)* One of the most widely read authors of romantic fiction in English literature. Died prematurely, of an illness. Never married. Her novels have rarely been out of print to this day.

* *Elinor and Marianne* – revised and eventually published as **"Sense and Sensibility"**.

* *First Impressions* – revised and eventually published as **"Pride and Prejudice"**.

* *Susan* – working title of **"Northanger Abbey"** published posthumously.

The Baroda Pearls

A tale of war, murder, greed, lust and romance... and a famous string of pearls.

1/8

The tumultuous 20th century was fizzling out, like a spectacular fire-cracker spewing out the dying embers of its explosive payload. Sergei Androvich was enjoying a life of self-indulgent decadence at his luxury villa in Odessa, on the Black Sea. Like several other fabulously rich high-profile Russians, he had made a staggering fortune out of the collapse of the Soviet Union through cheap acquisition of state-run industries.

Androvich had become an obsessive collector of art and rare gems. His private collection would make any international gallery curator drool. Many pieces were unsaleable, notably the Raphael 'Portrait of a Young Man' – unseen by anyone for over fifty years since hanging in Hitler's drawing room.

Another of his prized possessions was a necklace – a single string of 36 phenomenally large, equal-sized, perfect white pearls, selected from the famous Baroda Pearl Necklace owned once by a Gaikwad Maharaja, who squirreled it out of India to his love-nest in Monte Carlo before the end of the British Raj. Its ornate diamond clasp was fashioned and signed by Cartier.

One particular balmy evening, Sergei was entertaining a young lady at his villa. The girl was hand-picked by the escort agency he himself bankrolled. His plans for her would enable him to wallow in the obscene opulence of his own wealth.

He brought the necklace up from his basement strongroom, and fitted it around the naked girl's neck. The pearls gleamed against her flawless olive skin, and danced in perfect step with her long lustrous black hair and hazel-green eyes. His fetishistic impulses would soon involve him kissing and caressing her neck, shoulders and breasts, using the pearls between his lips. Then, he would be twisting the string with his fingers as if to strangle the girl, and she would doubtless gasp as a result of the tightening tourniquet. Thus aroused by the perverted symbolism of the power of riches, he would indulge himself with her body, in simple animal lust.

Androvich broke into a leering self-satisfied smile, and began undressing himself. Seconds later, he lay dead.

He would have had no idea what hit him. The hired squeeze grabbed her clothes and fled, scared out of her wits. She was never again seen in the Ukraine. The tall, athletic, fair-haired assassin disassembled her rifle and slipped away, as stealthily as she had arrived, undetected by the estate's security system, and reasonably confident that her contract had been honoured.

You cannot attain mega-tycoon status without making one or two enemies.

2/8

In what is now known as Kosovo, unspeakable atrocities were being committed on innocent civilians in the name of political ambition and ethnic 'cleansing'.

John's unit, part of the United Nations peace-keeping force, had for some weeks been patrolling the streets around Pristina, the main city. Things were relatively quiet, and there was a mood of optimism amongst both the residents, and the Albanian and U.N. troops who were encouraged to fraternise with the local people.

Despite living under a terrible cloud of danger and uncertainty, life went on, to some extent at least. People ate, drank, shopped, socialised, cheated on their partners, watched TV and argued about celebrities – all the things normal people do all the time. Many establishments stayed open for 'business as usual' – the oldest profession in the world, to mention just one.

On the edge of the Dardani district, just off the highway south towards Macedonia, was a brothel. Despite its all-encompassing name 'Club Rotterdam', it made no attempt to disguise what the entertainment was. And apparently there were no restrictions on what services could be made available, as long as enough dinars were forthcoming, or any other international currency, come to that.

John was a young man and it seemed a long, long time since he had been with any women back in the west. Local girls were notoriously difficult to get to know – the language barrier being the least of the problems. Albanian-Kosovan families robustly protected their daughters from troops of any kind.

Among the various multi-national agencies there was precious little available talent either, and those worth considering were generally too pre-occupied with some emergency to have time to socialise. Allison, one of the aid workers alongside John's unit, he certainly found attractive. But she took her responsibilities far too seriously to entertain any thoughts of dalliance, and particularly not with anyone in the military, for whom she had declared herself off-limits on several occasions.

Other guys seemed to be flocking shamelessly to Club Rotterdam. Why shouldn't John?

3/8

"Am Tatiana. You like?" There wasn't much not to like about Tatiana, was John's immediate opinion. She had youthful beauty, a flawless olive complexion and a perfect figure. She was dressed in an expensive-looking black leather shirt-dress which accentuated her cleavage and rode high on her thighs. Simple slip-on heeled sandals emphasised the shapeliness of her legs. Flowing black hair glistened with a lustre which belied the war-torn environment in which she lived and survived. John was particularly impressed by the presumably cheap, white plastic bead necklace she wore. It provided such eye-catching contrast.

John was a soldier. He was ready to kill the enemy, but underneath, he was a good and conscientious person, always ready to make friends, and reluctant to take advantage of anyone. But when it came to a woman in black leather, he was a slightly different animal. Any woman thus attired just seemed to be saying to him, "Please fuck me."

"I like very much," John replied. "I am John."

Tatiana remained impassive. "Want massage, in price pay. Want blojo 30 dinar extra, front hole 100 dinar, back hole 200 dinar. Bareback extra. You want?"

'So, romance is not dead,' thought John.

He actually wanted to slowly remove her shirt, fondle her breasts as they became more and more exposed, play with her nipples using his lips and tongue, slide his hand down the front of her panties, finger what he felt certain would be a smoothly shaven pussy – all manner of recognised foreplay activities, in fact. But how does one communicate that desire to a stranger who is probably working under duress, and whose command of the English language has progressed little further than 'front hole', 'back hole' and their associated worth in local currency? He gave it a try, though.

Tatiana was understandably reluctant to negotiate anything she didn't fully understand. Pluckily, she strove to pin down John's requirements: "Want fuck front hole? Tatiana good fuck. You like. Sure."

"Sure," sighed John, abandoning any more attempts to communicate. He counted out 100 dinars.

Two days later, Club Rotterdam was razed to the ground by Serbian communist tanks. There were no surviving occupants. Tatiana, or whatever might have been her real name, became another statistic in the ongoing horror story of man's inhumanity to man.

4/8

John had been doing a stint at the misplaced persons centre they had rigged up in the City Hall. He found sharing the traumatic experiences of people desperately seeking their lost loved ones could almost be as stressful as dealing with the heat of battle.

A swarthy middle-aged man with a black moustache had approached him. He spoke English well, with an east-European accent. Had anyone seen his daughter? Her last known location was the Dardani district. John checked the lists. No, no one of that name. Could the man provide a description? Yes, he could – he had a photograph. John's heart sank. It was 'Tatiana'.

At the temporary morgue, retrieved bodies and body-parts were photographed and roughly catalogued. There was neither time nor resources for much more detailed identification. John had already checked, and had not seen the girl there, although, distressingly, most of the exhibits were unrecognisable anyway. He reasoned it was better for the man to go there and verify it for himself, rather than being told that a soldier recognised his daughter because she worked in a knocking shop.

It was getting late. John headed off to his makeshift billet. A jeep pulled up alongside as he walked.

"Get in," the single occupant, a tall athletic-bodied young woman called across. She wore the uniform of a U.N. Police Officer, her light-blue beret, with its 'world map' motif, perched jauntily over her cropped fair hair.

John was trained to be wary of stepping anywhere beyond his predefined route. He was therefore reluctant to do her bidding, even though an invitation like that from someone who personified sex-on-legs was hard to turn down. "And you are...?" he cursorily checked.

"Get in," she repeated, politely, but in a tone of diminishing patience.

Sheepishly, John got in. "Sorry, er... Officer. Just, I don't get chatted up by too many women UNPOLs."

"Problem with that, Private Baines?"

She knew his name? Was he in some shit? But, hell, she was sexy, her piercing blue eyes looking as though she'd just breezed off a Hollywood film set rather than a dusty road pock-marked by shelling. "No problem, er... Officer."

"Good," she said. "Welcome to the modern world. Call me Nicki. Now shut up for a minute, I'll drive you home."

5/8

The UN had commandeered floors in several of the city hotels, and John was fortunate to have a small, though rather dingy single room to himself. "Welcome to the honeymoon suite," he quipped.

Nicki didn't reply, but took a sheet from her attaché case. "Recognise this man?" she asked, showing John the picture of a swarthy middle-aged man with a black moustache. John recounted his meeting with the man, who had claimed he was from Moldova.

"And had you ever come across the girl in his photo?"

John wondered briefly whether Nicki's wording was deliberately suggestive. "No," he replied, economising on truth.

"You want to pull down your pants and show me your ass?" Nicki asked, quite matter-of-factly.

John was momentarily taken aback. Ironically, that was the very question he had longed to ask her, but hardly dared to.

"Shouldn't we have a drink first, perhaps, Nicki?" he tentatively suggested.

She produced another photograph from the case, continuing: "Only... I wanted to compare it to this one."

John peered into the gaping chasm of his undoing – a hidden cam at the Club Rotterdam had captured him in flagrante delicto. There was no weedling out of it. John came clean about everything, feebly offering his excuse that he didn't want the man to know about his daughter's activities.

"Very noble of you," said Nicki sardonically. "Now then, listen up. Your grieving Moldovan father is a Russian master-criminal, has no children, is a KGB hitman and is wanted by law enforcement agencies world-wide. Did you not wonder why he spoke good English and his grown 'daughter' didn't? You may even now be on his hit-list, so if you meet him again, shoot first and ask questions later, Ok? Oh yes, and... was the girl any good?"

A stun grenade would probably have had the same effect. John tried to take it all in, but before thinking to ask what a KGB hitman was doing in a UN controlled war-zone and what it had to do with a woman UNPOL officer, he observed Nicki unbuttoning her shirt.

She was clearly a devotee of the 'girls on top'

principle, unbelting John's pants, letting them fall with his shorts around his ankles, then shoving him backwards onto the chair. She completed stripping herself, then sat astride his lap, thrusting her breasts into his face. John, an athletic type himself, felt no urge to resist, deciding to take his chances of being ravished by the hottest of Amazons he was likely ever to get lucky with. "Make the most of it, mate," he said to himself.

As they dressed afterwards, Nicki said: "John, be a sweetie and pop down to the kitchen and get us a cup of green tea, with lemon and honey."

John doubted the catering would stretch to it, but went as bid. And while he spent that time, she searched his room, and every bag, holdall and rucksack. She didn't find what she was looking for, and neither could John find any green tea, nor his latest lover by the time he got back to the room.

6/8

Allison lost patience. "These people need fresh water, and they need it now, not tomorrow, not next week... get out of my way, I'll fetch the fucking stuff myself!" Allison could be very single-minded at times. She heaved the container onto her shoulder and strode purposefully across the tarmac strip towards the bowser.

"Oh shit. Stupid woman," thought John – an opinion shared with just about everyone else at that moment. They shouted to her, but there was little anyone could do – she was in the open and a sitting duck for the sniper that had been spotted in the building opposite. "Hell," resolved John, "I'm going to do at least something gallant in my life. Probably get killed in the process... shit... now or never..." and he ran.

He dived at her like he was back in his school rugby team, cutting off a try attempt by the enemy school's speedy wing threequarter. The tackle was a bit high, but effective. They both hit the deck, painfully, and rolled. John managed to direct the tumble so that they ended lengthwise in the culvert by a post at the side of the road. The high kerbstone gave them some cover from the sniper's line of fire.

Allison fumed. "You idiot! You clown! What do you think you're doing? Will you please get off me this minute!!" She tried to sit up, using the wooden post to support herself. John immediately pushed her back down, smothering her in a most ungentlemanly fashion to stop her retrying. A split second later, the bullet from a high-powered Zastava sniper rifle shattered the five by five wooden post, at the height Allison's head would have been. They both were showered in debris.

Allison gasped in shock and horror. Sometimes it takes such a near miss to remind us of one's mortality, like falling asleep at the wheel and waking up bumping along the grass verge, rather than not waking up at all. She looked into John's eyes – they were that close, there was little else to look into. She blinked.

"Thanks for saving my life," Allison said calmly and collectedly, after coming to her senses.

"Pleasure," said John, tersely.

"And sorry I made you risk your own."

"No prob."

"What do we do now?"

"Nothing," said John. "Just be patient. Snipers know that sooner or later their target will decide it's safe to put their head up again. But he knows our guys will be trying to pinpoint where he is, so he won't want to hang around forever. You've just got to out-stay him. Lay still. Keep calm."

John was actually quite contented. He was finally atop Allison, whose parted legs had afforded him a snug position below the kerb-line, cushioned from the stone by her thighs. He had her shoulders pinned to the ground to stop her bobbing up again, and her torn uniform gave him a welcome view of her rather pretty lacy bra and the curves of her breasts.

They lay, quiet in the drain. Cold dirty water, carrying sodden litter and sludge trickled beneath them and was gradually soaking them both. The stones were hard and rough, and the smell was anything but fresh. And in that antithesis of a romantic setting, Allison whispered, "Come here often?"

John's heart skipped a beat. Had he at last pierced the body-armour of Allison's heart? Apparently, she was human after all – and sexy when she wanted to be, reasoned John, taking logical thought progression forward in ridiculously quick steps.

"Only in the mating season," he replied. "You?"

"Only when I'm made to lie in a cold wet filthy ditch underneath a randy squaddie."

"What makes you think I'm randy?" John asked, feigning innocence.

"Well, I assume that's not a gun sticking into my tummy."

John realised the source of Allison's discomfort was his radio, holstered to his belt. But he chose to let the comment ride. Smiling, he continued the repartee: "Doing anything after work?"

"Yes," said Allison. "A hot shower, washing this shit out of my hair, putting on some clean dry clothes and having a glass of wine."

"Oh, you like wine? Fancy a pint of the local Riesling? It's very acceptable, I hear."

"Chateau Lafite for me, preferably a '75," Allison replied with straight face.

"I prefer the '98 myself," said John, trying to sound like James Bond.

"Asshole. You've never had a decent glass of wine in your life – you're all mouth and trousers."

7/8

John felt that any barriers between them were well and truly breached. He was confident that stealing a kiss would not send her into indignant hysterics. So he did. She didn't reciprocate with much passion, but that was hardly surprising given their grim situation. Then after a short awkward silence, Allison asked, "Is that the best you can do?"

John didn't need any more green lights. He wasn't bothered about an ensuing court martial accusing him of civilian assault or something.

He could always claim he needed to keep the panic-stricken woman calm by any means available – tenuous defence but viable. A Land Rover skidded to a halt nearby.

With his free right hand, John tenderly stroked the exposed breast which had been tantalising him for so long, and was about to kiss her more passionately when a familiar-sounding female voice broke the silence: "You two having fun down there?"

It was Nicki, in fatigues rather than her police uniform, and brandishing a Kalashnikov.

"Get down!" John shouted. "There's a sniper in the building opposite..."

"Was," said the tall athletic blonde. "He had an accident. Broken neck, it seems. Amateur."

"But... how? You?"

Nicki suddenly sounded menacing. "John, don't get up. I only have a short time before the rest of your motley oppos get here. I count to five and the girl dies. You can blame the sniper. But you can change all that. John, where are the pearls? One..."

"Pearls? What pearls?" John's pathetic response sounded exactly like what it was – a hackneyed melodramatic effort to buy time.

"Two..."

Allison interjected, with justifiable concern. "John? What's she talking about? What pearls?"

"Three..."

There was no way John could deploy his firearm, or indeed, offer any effective combat from the position he was in.

"Four..."

So he did his best to cover Allison – sheer instinct. She was a totally innocent victim of circumstance, he less innocent, but clearly the cause of their joint predicament. He held his breath, and prayed.

But 'five' never came. Instead, there was a thud, and the tall, athletic, fair-haired assassin crumpled in a heap, blood oozing fast from her left temple.

"You guys Ok?" asked the swarthy man with the black moustache, putting away his pistol.

"And you are...?" John enquired, trying to sound cool, and determined to check people's credentials more thoroughly from now on.

The man readily introduced himself, thrusting his ID badge towards John: "Francis Dick, Interpol. Sorry I had to put on the grieving father act the other day. Couldn't afford to spook you in case you were in cahoots with this one," nodding towards the ground. "Look, get your arses over to Medical, have yourselves checked out. I'll take care of things here. Catch up with you in a while."

8/8

In less troubled times, it would have been classed as quite a plush hotel bar. Right now, there were boxes piled here and there, broken furnishings and shabby carpets. Bar stocks were desperately low. John and Francis downed some unspecified beer from plastic cups. The Interpol agent explained how he had tailed Irma Lakshmi, aka Nicki and various other false names, across half of Europe investigating multiple contract killings. John asked what had brought the deadly assassin to Pristina.

"She got greedy," Francis explained. "After taking out a rich Russian in the Ukraine, she collected her fee, but found out some call-girl had benefited by making off with a valuable pearl necklace. She traced the girl to here, and found her working at the Club Rotterdam. The Serbs flattened the place before Irma had a chance to recover the pearls. So she followed up leads of who the girl might have passed them on to. You, for instance."

Freshened up, Allison joined them, none the worse for wear except for a few bruises and grazes. To John, she looked radiant. He was in love.

They told Allison about Irma, and Tatiana, and the priceless pearls. To boost his chances of making it long-term with Allison, John decided not to mention too much detail about his actual liaisons with the two women.

In return, Allison decided not to mention anything about the string of 'white beads' she had found in the rubble at Dardani, while supporting the rescue operations. Or putting them in a biscuit tin, intending eventually to take them to the young children at the refugee centre to play with.

End.

Afterburn: A few years into the new millennium, in April 2007, a necklace made from the original Baroda Pearls mysteriously turned up at Christie's in New York. It sold at auction for over $7 million – a world record.

The Pornbroker's Assistant

Jimmy gets some film work. But what sort of movie is it...?

1/5

Jimmy always had a thing about film photography. As a young lad in Manchester, he watched old movies at the Withington Scala, not for their story, action or dialogue, but for the cinematography. He drooled over John Ford's depiction of the rugged Utah-Arizona landscape filmed through a barn door in 'The Searchers', and Carol Reed's quirky steep-angle shots of post-war Vienna's rain-soaked cobbled streets in 'The Third Man'. They were film director gods, and Jimmy idolised them.

He hankered to be a director himself, but it was a job requiring a high level of man (and woman) management skill, whereas zoom factors, aperture settings, soft focus, tripod alignment and chromatic aberration were technical issues which he could chat about with consummate ease. Chat, however, not liable to procure him many girlfriends.

After graduating with a photography degree, Jimmy freelanced doing stills and video for weddings and similar functions. Ironically, his innovative talents were not always totally appreciated. Several brides had been disappointed with his unconventional style, preferring a more traditional wedding album, with people posing formally in-a-row-smiling, rather than being shot from behind looking back over their shoulder, and the like.

He also managed to get work for an advertising agency, and at one point excitedly submitted footage for a toothpaste commercial. It featured his synchronisation of the glint in a hunky would-be suitor's eye with the sparkle of a warm ray of sunlight falling upon the open mouth of the girl with the perfect teeth, who supposedly used the toiletry product in question.

The shot, never aired, was consigned to the cutting-room floor. And Jimmy's proud mum had sat in vain through several episodes of Coronation Street just to catch the ad.

But America was where it was at, so Jimmy packed his bags. Well, bag... and camera case. His eventual ambition was Hollywood, but for the moment, his finances stretched only to a temporary work permit, and a flight to the Big Apple.

2/5

Jimmy soon knew he had made the right

decision. After just a few days in town, at a bar in Greenwich Village, a tall black man of Rastafarian persuasion eyed him up and down through dilated pupils, approached, and addressed him.

"Youz dat limey dude wid da fancy Nikon?"

Jimmy figured obviously he had been spotted out and about Manhattan with his camera, capturing the stark contrast between the uncompromising downtown scrapers and the laid-back sprawl of the 'Village'. And his new-found friend clearly recognised his brand of equipment.

"Yes. Hi. James Woodbridge. You must have seen me photographing these wonderful streets. Can I buy you a drink?" Jimmy hoped it wouldn't amount to anything too expensive.

"Be allowin me, dude," offered Bruno, the man with the dreadlocks. He signalled to the barman, who duly delivered a concoction Jimmy didn't recognise, but swigged to be polite with a grateful Mancunian 'Cheers!'

"Be lettin me cut to da quick, Jimbo. You handle a Pee Em Dubya Tree Hunderd?" The New Yorker was hardly talking the Queen's English, but it was Jimmy's language.

"The PMW-300?" Jimmy enthused. "The new Sony XDCAM with the EX mount lens system?

Sure thing. Best cam around for HD!" Jimmy had never used one – it was way out of his price range. But he was confident he could handle one, given half a chance.

"Hmm..." Bruno deliberated. "Be lettin me see... Jimbo, if youz lookin to hit da movie scene big time, I be knowin a certain top dude... be excusin me while I make a call." Jimmy couldn't believe his luck.

Bruno was a fixer. He had a million contacts in New York, and was able to supply anybody with almost anything, including TVs, automobiles, cell phones, and Bob Marley memorabilia. And girls, and various substances... And in Jimmy's case, an expert familiar with the particular model of movie camera Bruno had recently 'acquired' for Luigi, his 'top dude' regular client.

They walked the couple of blocks to a backroom studio in a seedy apartment building owned and managed by Luigi's dubious organisation.

3/5

"Mr. Luigi, sir, this here's Jimbo the limey I wuz bein tellin you bout. He one of Yeurop's finest camera monkeys. What he done know bout video shit aint worth shit. And he can handle this here Pee Em Dubya Tree Hunderd like he wuz shellin peas."

Luigi was broad shouldered, shaven-headed, and looked like he was made of granite. And according to Bruno, as Jimmy learnt during the short journey from the bar, no one messed with Luigi. No one. Bruno didn't mention what happened to Luigi's previous lens-man who had absconded with the last camera.

Luigi eyed both Jimmy and Bruno with suspicion. "You fucken with me, Bruno? This kid looks wet behind the ears."

Jimmy's resolve was beginning to falter.

As if to clarify, Luigi added: "I ain't splashing a thousand fucken bucks a week on some mutherfucken amateur."

Jimmy's resolve perked back up. He wondered if he had heard right. Did Luigi say 'a thousand... a week'?

The big man reluctantly summoned his assistant. "Dolores!" Then, turning to Jimmy, warned: "And kid, fuck up and I'll spread your limey ass all over the fucken street." No pressure then.

The unflappable Dolores, only in her twenties, was a world-weary export of New Jersey. She responded to the summons, busily doing what she normally was – filing her nails.

Jimmy immediately admired how photogenic she was, despite being imperfectly proportioned, mousy haired and with character lines around her eyes. And flat heels did nothing to enhance her appeal in a fashion-model sense. But Jimmy visually framed only the beauty within, and was instantly smitten.

"Dolores. Fix the limey up with a room out front. We start shooting in the morning. Angie's booked and Dirk fucken Dagwell should be here 9 am."

"Dirk Dagwell?" Dolores remarked. "Sheesh. Really?"

Jimmy tried to recall where he had heard the name before. It was very similar to that of a famously well-endowed male porn actor, but probably someone entirely different.

Dolores showed Jimmy to his accommodation. "Here's your lil room, Mr Woodbridge." Then, handing him the case of Sony equipment supplied by Bruno, she added, "You'll be needing these gizmos in the morning."

"Friends call me Woody," Jimmy ventured speculatively, but without any obvious reaction.

"This kit is the real deal, huh?" she asked, out of polite curiosity.

"Absolutely," Jimmy answered. "The PMW

range is ideal if you want a camera suitable for both shoulder mounting and normal ENG functions."

"No shit?" Dolores exclaimed. "Woody, you sure talk sweet."

Jimmy and Dolores could hardly have come from more dissimilar backgrounds, but somehow Jimmy felt hugely attracted to her uniqueness, openness, and dry wit. But Dolores was more than just streetwise. She was a woman, and could already sense the way things would go.

Jimmy checked Bruno's gear, and was relieved to find a manual. He would have time to get more familiar with the controls and actually check that everything functioned. But he also needed to know a bit more about what was required of him. He managed to intercept Dolores as she headed for the door.

"Er, Dolores. Any idea what sort of filming this is tomorrow? Like, who is the director?"

Dolores looked blank. "Director? It ain't Gone With the Wind, Woody. It's a porno. And it's your show." And, in response to Jimmy's nervous expression, "Hell, you done loads of porn shoots back in Ingerland... ain't you Woody?"

"Er... yeah. Sure... 'Cos I have." Three things

came to Jimmy's mind. One: how do I do a porn shoot? Two: a thousand bucks a week. Three: what am I going to tell my mum when I write home? Then, quickly following, a fourth thing: Jimmy's ass spread all over the street.

"I'll be around if you need me, hun," Dolores reassured him.

"On set?" Jimmy asked.

"Around, ok? I'm continuity, and coffee. See ya in the morning Woody." And Jimmy was left with his thoughts, not least of which was why a porn flick needed a continuity girl.

4/5

Morning arrived, as did Angie ("Busty") McClusky. She was expected to be late, like always, but she had got the time wrong. She sat busily overdoing her make-up.

Dirk Dagwell appeared soon afterwards. The two leads, having worked together on previous occasions, nodded at each other begrudgingly. Jimmy, concerned about the chemistry between his stars, eyed Dolores. She whispered, "They hate each other, but don't worry, Woody... it'll be fine."

Jimmy took a deep breath, then the plunge. "Ok if we get started, guys?"

Dirk and Angie started stripping off, as they had done on film sets countless times, totally oblivious of decorum.

"No, no, wait." Jimmy stopped them. "Miss McClusky – you are in bed, a silky nightie is slipping off your shoulders... you're just waking from your night's sleep, rubbing your eyes... The half-light catches your facial profile and the curve of your cleavage... A shadow moves ominously across your face – that's Dolores drawing a towel across the spot-beam... And you open your eyes wider in shock. Your mouth drops open, just a fraction – Dolores will gloss the lower lip, I'll get a nice soft focus glimmer from it as it trembles... You see the intruder, and it has filled you with a mixture of fear and desire. You shrink away...

"Dirk – I want you initially clothed, something dark, brooding. And a trilby hat if there's one in wardrobe... You stand upright, tall, and looking mean and menacing – I'll lie between your feet and shoot you from the floor, elongate the perspective to broaden your shoulders and turn up the curvature of your snarling lip... oh yes, and accentuate the bulge in your pants... You've just broken in to settle an old score, and you are going to get your way, no matter what."

Angie and Dirk looked at each other disbelievingly. They were thinking the same thing. He expects us to act??? Dolores brought some coffee.

By mid-morning, Jimmy had filled several memory cards with usable foreplay footage, including Dirk's kissing of Angie's shoulderblade while Dolores held Angie's vibrator to Jimmy's lens-hood, creating on film a unique shivery effect representing Angie's sensations.

It was time for the movie's climax, so to speak.

Jimmy decided to splice a number of ultra-short sequences together, each teasingly cutting off at a critical moment, like just as hands were moving across a thigh, or lips down a chest, each about to trespass into forbidden territory... and a slo-mo of Dolores' pretty forefinger sliding sensuously along the longest schlong in show business, towards where a drop of watered glycerine convincingly faked reality.

Jimmy was practically joining the action himself. Shots from the top, shots from the bottom, shots between bodies about to engage, and, using Dolores' make-up mirror taped to his male lead's tummy, a shot down Dirk's dick, with a zoom into a bath-soap frothed-up Angie beckoning it towards her. And with Angie genuinely enjoying the taste of it, even the squirty salad-dressing from the kitchen became a useful prop, avoiding the danger of over-stretching her acting ability.

So many scenes. So many takes. And with Dirk's dick up and down, Jimmy got to appreciate the importance of a continuity girl, or 'fluffer', to use the industry vernacular. He was pleased with his work, and pleased he hadn't felt any arousal, which would have been very unprofessional.

He did feel guilty though. Guilty of envy. Dolores had been working her magic keeping Dirk interested. But all Jimmy got was coffee.

5/5

By midweek, Jimmy and Dolores had enough new material in the can to put several films together. They uploaded "The Intruder", "Intruder 2", and "Return of the Intruder" to the streaming company. Jimmy's work was out on the net!

Jimmy was hopeful that Luigi, due to look in for a progress meeting, would be pleased. But when the big man of granite did look in, his mood was not good.

"What in fuck's name is this crap on our pay channel? Is this what you fucken wasters have been doing on my fucken time all fucken week? I got a public, paying through the ass for porn, not art-house shit. Guys want stuff to jerk off to, not Mary fucken Poppins.

"I'll give you to Friday. More ass. Less fart-ass. Geddit?"

As the boss was storming out, Dolores spoke up. She was used to Luigi's bluster. "Luigi, I just got Toosday's figures off the pooter. Fourteen thousand log-ons, average connection time eighteen minutes - that's sixty-seven percent up on last week's. We're getting more guys, and they're watching for longer."

Luigi quickly converted connection times into revenue. "Ha!" he sneered. Conceding an argument was not his style. "Make fucken sure that trend stays firm," adding, with a miserable attempt at humour, "firmer than Dagwell's fucken dick, anyhow." He slammed the door behind him.

Dolores was the first to break the silence. "He likes you, Woody."

By the end of the week, the team had produced a whole series of minimalist-dialog high-impact camera-work pornos, the log-ons and connection times were increasing exponentially, and experts within the industry were talking.

Jimmy sat alone in the studio with a beer, and wrote home: 'Hi Mum. Arrived safely. People here really friendly. Got some work, filming a silly romance. Pay is quite good. Met a girl.

You'd like her. Hope your bunions are better. Love James'.

He went to his 'lil' room, thinking about Dolores. It wasn't until after he'd cleaned his teeth, undressed and got into his pyjamas, that he discovered his bed was already occupied. The naked Dolores, laying on her side, elbow on pillow, hand supporting her head, calmly chirped "Hello Woody."

Jimmy had spent a week practically in bed with an overdeveloped and oversexed porn actress without any significant feelings. But up against Dolores' warm body he felt nothing but ecstasy. What a difference love and affection can make between the sheets.

Dolores' petite rounded breasts were no match for Busty McClusky's, and neither was Jimmy blessed with tackle anything like as impressive as Dirk Dagwell's. But as he caressed her, she gasped each time her nipples, like bullets, flicked under his palms. And as he stroked her mound, brushing the tiny tufts of trimmed hair with his fingers she moaned softly and clenched her pelvic muscles.

And he realised that it was the mutual interaction of 'stimulus and response', and not porn's one-way 'perform and be watched', which quintessentially defines the sensual pleasure of sex.

"Dolores. I think you're wonderful. I just love you to bits. Why can't I capture you on a Stratasys Polyjet 3-d printer and have you by me all the time?"

"Shit, Woody. You sure talk sweet."

End.

The 2012 Sex Olympics

London 2012. Svetlana goes for gold. Terry assists.

1/3

The build-up to the 2012 London Olympics involved an incredible organisational effort to ensure infrastructure and facilities would afford optimum security, accessibility, and comfort for competitors, officials, media and spectators alike.

The 'Olympic Village', for housing teams from all nations, was a new multistory, hi-tech apartment block, ultimately destined to be sold off as living accommodation for the general public. To ensure a safe and secure environment for food preparation, given the stringent dietary requirements of athletes, a centralised catering service was laid on, allowing the builders to get away with not having to provide kitchen facilities in each apartment. Personally, I couldn't be doing without my cheese toasties in the middle of the night. But then, I didn't qualify for the Olympics anyway. Shut up.

Bedrooms, however, were an obvious necessity. And no one was naive enough to imagine beds would not get shared. Indeed, the Olympic Committee, with commendable vision, fully expected a great deal of 'sharing', given the whole block would be full of fit, strapping, hormone-crazed human specimens in the prime of life. In view of this, the organisers made freely available a supply of high-specification condoms, all specially packaged. With meticulous attention to detail, their logo was printed on each packet, with of course, the accompanying Olympic motto: "Citius, Altius, Fortius". Which, as we all know, is Latin for "Faster... Higher... Stronger..." Mmm...

One may think such bedroom exertions would be detrimental to an athlete's chances of success in an upcoming competition. But, while having it off just before your event is not considered tactically prudent on the grounds of one's diminished energy reserves, or being totally knackered, it is generally accepted, though the area is sadly lacking in research, that performing in the bedroom the night before does little to affect performance in the stadium the following day. Indeed, sexual activity increases testosterone levels in men, thus actually enhancing their competitiveness.

And in any case, apparently, sex doesn't use up a vast amount of energy – a commonly held critique I have heard voiced by several disgruntled female acquaintances. In fact, on average, according to reliable scientific sources, people only burn off 50 calories per bonk – bad news for those who exploit such occasions to justify woofing down a bar of Cadburys afterwards. Yes, you.

Dr Hans Brügger, an eminent sports physician famously reported that, as a result of heightened bodily responsiveness, women get better results in competition after orgasm, and the more orgasms, the more chances of winning a medal. Well, if that's true, I'm prepared to believe that a good number of female athletes would willingly put in the work and make the sacrifice for team and country. But one must not rule out the greater likelihood that the eminent sports physician in question was simply trying to improve his own chances of getting his leg over. And we're not talking about high jump.

Grigor, the old-guard-soviet coach for the Danzakhstan contingent, did not share my cynical view. Set on achieving results by fair means or foul, he had already been in trouble with the authorities for use of illegal equipment and banned substances. Desperate to enhance performance in an undetectable way, he now was intent on making the most of the body's natural mechanisms, and readily took on board the eminent Dr Brügger's theories. The lithe and shapely Svetlana was Danzakhstan's main medal hope in the Taekwondo 69kg category, and Grigor was determined to get the very ultimate effort out of his prized athlete. He set about trying to convince her that orgasms spelt medals.

"But, Grigor, boyfriend driving tractor back in homeland," Svetlana protested.

"At this level, Svetlana girl, hundredth of second speed, millimetre of accuracy, or microgram of weight behind secret rabbit punch when referee blink, make all difference between gold, and kaputshit. Think of Mother Country, Svetlana, you have duty."

"But, Grigor..."

"Who needs boyfriend, Svetlana girl," the wizened old coach interrupted, "this London – capital of decadent Western cesspit-world. Everything available at touch of button. No need boyfriend. I arrange service call, 9pm tonight. Be ready. Lay back and think of Danzakhstan."

2/3

Terry was a down-to-earth Eastender and versatile odd-job man. He had relished the opportunity of work when the Olympics were awarded to London, and was delighted that the main venue site was chosen to be Stratford – Terry's stomping ground. He had got himself into the pool of contractors employed to sort out teething problems with the newly completed accommodation block, and deal with ongoing maintenance issues during the Games. He was on late shift, and checking the smoke alarms in D-Wing.

"Yes, who is it?" called Svetlana, a little startled by the ringing of her door-bell. It was only 8.15pm.

"Maintenance," Terry sang back. "Just a service call."

Svetlana opened her door. "But you early," she said, looking him up and down. He was in overalls, a flat cap, and displayed on his face two days of unattended stubble. Svetlana was pleasantly surprised – she had feared that her arranged date would be some suited pretty-boy from the city, but Terry uncannily reminded her of Dmitri, her beefy, straightforward, farm-working lover back home. Her heart warmed accordingly.

"Nah, a bit late, to be 'onest, luv," Terry apologised, "I've got all of D-block to get through yet."

"Bozemoy!" cried Svetlana, (which was Danzakhstani for 'My Goodness'). "What strength you must have!"

Terry was used to everyone in the block not being able to understand one another. "Strenfth? No, luv. This job I jus' need to find the right buttons to press," he explained.

"I show you button to press," Svetlana said, slipping off her robe, eager to get on with it. Then, as naked as a Danzakhstani dumpling-frog, she leapt on him, her powerful thighs locking round his waist, in a move not recognised by any known Taikwondo training manual. They fell heavily onto the bed, and there was the ominous sound of timber creaking.

"That's another cross-support frame gone," Terry thought to himself, while still, though only just, in maintenance mode.

"Oh Dmitri," Svetlana sighed, hurriedly removing the workman's overalls and delving into Terry's underpants. "Let Svetti feel your passion swelling... Oh my Dmitri... My lovey dovey big cock man..."

"Steady on, luv," Terry half-heartedly complained, "and it's Terry, actually, ooh... er... that's nice..."

3/3

Svetlana was unsure whether it was the stimulating effect of Terry's bristly chin grinding on her smoothly-shaven vulva, the novel use of his buzzing circuit tester checking out the electrical continuity of her clit ring, or the good old-fashioned shafting from his lovey dovey big cock, but she was well satisfied, and had achieved her required quota of orgasms.

"Sorry to love-ya an' leave-ya, doll," Terry said, genuinely apologetic, "but I need to get me round done or I'll be in shit street."

She lay back, wondering in what part of London Shit Street might be, and dreaming of Dmitri and Olympic Gold. "You good. I get Grigor to send for you again before next Taikwondo bout."

Terry didn't have a clue what she was on about, but wished her best of luck in her contest the next day.

"I confident now," Svetlana purred. "I kick crap out of Armenian douchebag tomorrow. No problems."

As Terry walked back past the security desk, he noticed a tall, slim young man in a smart suit and Gucci shoes, remonstrating with the duty officer that he needed access to visit a client in D-Wing. Terry thought to himself, "You may be the one with a sharp whistle, mate, but I'm the one whose got one of these," referring to the ID card dangling on a cord around his neck.

Danzakhstan failed to progress further than the first round in the women's Taekwondo 69kg. category, so the eminent sports physician's theory remained unproven. One cannot discount the possibility, however, that the douchebag from Armenia had somehow managed to surpass even Svetlana's climax count the night before.

Whether she did, or nay, the fact is that GB women achieved a record number of podium places – a fact which did not go unobserved by a Mrs Vera Huggett, one of the contract cleaners, who commented to a Daily Mail reporter that the number of discarded Olympic condom packets in the bins of the Team GB women exceeded the total of all the other nations put together.

The End. National Anthem plays...

ABOUT...

This book's main story was originally titled 'The Great Splondini', but was changed to 'The Great Splonjini' to disambiguate it from the magician 'The Great Splendini', Woody Allen's film creation which came along in 2016.

Unix time is the number of seconds that have elapsed since the Unix epoch (1 January 1970), excluding leap seconds. Vast amounts of legacy software use a signed 32-bit integer to represent it, meaning that overflow will occur on 19 January 2038, and things will go seriously pear-shaped. Some applications that use future dates have already encountered the bug. Modern systems have been upgraded to use 64-bit integers. These will not overflow for 292 billion years. Don't hold your breath.

There really is a mobile snack bar called 'The Hound of the Basket Meals' which operates close to Hound Tor on Dartmoor. They serve over 17 sorts of tea, Brixham crab sandwiches and garlic hamburgers.

The International Olympic Committee apparently distributed 450,000 condoms to athletes at the Rio 2016 Olympic Village for the 17-day long Games – twice the number made available for London 2012.

www.ingramcontent.com/pod-product-compliance
Lightning Source LLC
Chambersburg PA
CBHW071615150726
48000CB00004B/1734